Praise for *Hidden in the Stars*

On top of being attacked and possibly maimed for life, Sophia Montgomery just learned she also lost her beloved mother in the attack, the mother who had lied her entire life about the grandmother standing in front of her now. Every quilt has a story, but will they be able to get this one to talk before it's too late and the killers return? Robin Caroll stitches together great suspense with a backing of romance and an edge of intrigue.

—Bonnie S. Calhoun, publisher of *Christian Fiction Online Magazine*, author of *Pieces of the Heart* and *Cooking the Books*

Other Books in the Quilts of Love Series

Beyond the Storm
Carolyn Zane

Tempest's Course
Lynette Sowell

A Wild Goose Chase Christmas
Jennifer AlLee

Scraps of Evidence
Barbara Cameron

Path of Freedom
Jennifer Hudson Taylor

A Sky Without Stars
Linda S. Clare

For Love of Eli
Loree Lough

A Promise in Pieces
Emily Wierenga

Threads of Hope
Christa Allan

A Stitch and a Prayer
Eva Gibson

A Healing Heart
Angela Breidenbach

Rival Hearts
Tara Randel

A Heartbeat Away
S. Dionne Moore

A Grand Design
Amber Stockton

Pieces of the Heart
Bonnie S. Calhoun

Hidden in the Stars
Robin Caroll

Pattern for Romance
Carla Olson Gade

Quilted by Christmas
Jodie Bailey

Raw Edges
Sandra D. Bricker

Swept Away
Laura V. Hilton & Cindy Loven

The Christmas Quilt
Vannetta Chapman

Masterpiece Marriage
Gina Welborn

Aloha Rose
Lisa Carter

A Stitch in Crime
Cathy Elliott

HIDDEN IN THE STARS

Quilts of Love Series

Robin Caroll

a novel approach to faith

Nashville

Hidden in the Stars

Copyright © 2014 by Robin C. Miller

ISBN-13: 978-1-4267-7360-0

Published by Abingdon Press, P.O. Box 801, Nashville, TN 37202

www.abingdonpress.com

Quilts of Love Macro Editor: Teri Wilhelms

Published in association with the Steve Laube Literary Agency

All rights reserved.

Library of Congress Cataloging-in-Publication Data

Caroll, Robin.
    Hidden in the stars / Robin Caroll.
        pages cm. — (Quilts of Love Series)
    ISBN 978-1-4267-7360-0 (binding: soft back/ trade/paperbck : alk. paper) 1. Life change events—Fiction. 2. Quilts—Fiction. 3. Healing-- Fiction. I. Title.
    PS3603.A7673H53 2014
    813'.6—dc23

                                                            2014008447

Printed in the United States of America

1 2 3 4 5 6 7 8 9 10 / 19 18 17 16 15 14

For Aunt Millicent
You are an example of beauty and grace.

Acknowledgments

Huge thanks to my editor, Ramona Richards, who believed in this story and helped bring it to light. I cannot thank you enough for your encouragement and ease in working with you. You are truly a blessing, and I feel so honored to get to work with you.

My thanks to the whole team at Abingdon for extending your talent and skill on my behalf. It's been a fun journey.

This book dealt with minute details regarding the medical field, ballet, and gymnastics. Huge thanks to the following people for sharing their knowledge with me: Dr. Skipper Bertrand, Tosca Lee, and Cara Putman. Any mistakes in the representation of details are mine, where I twisted in the best interest of my story.

My most heartfelt thanks to my awesome agent, Steve (HP) Laube, who knows when to step in to encourage and also to rein in. THANK YOU.

My extended family members are my biggest fans and greatest cheerleaders. Thank you for ALWAYS being in my corner: Mom, BB and Robert, Bek and Krys, Bubba and Lisa, Brandon, Rachel, and Aunt Millicent.

There is no way I could be inspired with stories without my girls—Emily Carol, Remington Case, and Isabella Co-Ceaux. I love each of you so much! Especially Remy and Bella, who survived many nights of cereal for dinner while I was writing. Thanks to my precious grandsons, Benton and Zayden—you are two of the coolest little dudes I know! Gran loves you!

My biggest shout out of appreciation is for my husband, Case. I can't thank you enough for helping me follow my dream. I could not do this without you, and I love you with all my heart.

Finally, all glory to my Lord and Savior, Jesus Christ. *I can do all things through Him who gives me strength.*

1

Beep. Beep. Beep.

What on earth was beeping so loudly? And annoyingly.

Sophia Montgomery blinked. Brightness burst through the slit she'd managed to force open. She squeezed her eyes shut tight again and sucked in air.

A strange stench curled her nostrils. It was almost rancid . . . disinfectant mingled with sweat. That made no sense . . .

There had been two men, banging at the door. Barging in. Knives. Big knives. Grabbing her by the hair and throwing her to the floor. She hit her head against the leg of the chair. The coppery-metallic taste of blood filled her mouth.

Sophia tried again to open her eyes. W-what? she mouthed, but not a sound escaped. Burning shards closed around her throat as she tried to swallow against a gravelly resistance. *Dear God, what's happening?*

"Shh. Don't try to talk," a woman's crackly voice soothed. "The doctor will be here in a moment."

Doctor? Sophia struggled to sit, but every muscle in her body resisted, a sure sign she'd overdone at practice. Gentle hands eased her still. A cool, damp cloth stroked her forehead.

"You thought you could get away with it?" one of the men had yelled. *His breath hissed against her face. Her neck.*

She blinked again, this time prepared for the light. Or so she thought. The brilliance burned. She moaned and snapped her eyes closed.

"I'm sorry. Let me turn down the light," the woman whispered in her guttural toned voice.

Click. The sound echoed in Sophia's head.

"There. This should be better."

Sophia tried squinting a third time. While still brighter than the darkness she'd been comfortable in, the light wasn't so searing. She barely made out the figure of a woman at her side, hunching over her bed.

Wait a minute. Something wasn't right. Where was she? *God?*

"Well, good morning," a man's cheerful voice boomed.

Still squinting, Sophia shifted her gaze to the voice's origin. The fuzzy silhouette moved close to her.

"I'm Dr. Rhoads. Nod if you can hear me okay."

A doctor? What was going on? She nodded and forced her eyes open wider as pain ricocheted around her shoulders.

"Good." Cold hands touched her forehead. She must have reacted in some way because he chuckled softly and said, "Sorry. Everyone says I have the coldest hands in Arkansas."

Arkansas . . . but she lived in Texas. Plano. Close to the gym where she trained.

Training! *Lord, what is going on?*

The doctor shined a light in her eyes, searing them with its intensity. She snapped them closed and turned her head, moving out of his hold.

"I know it's uncomfortable, but I had to check your pupils."

Sophia forced her eyes open, willing them to focus on the man. She could now see his white coat. Dark hair. Big smile—too big.

She opened her mouth to ask what was going on, but razors sliced inside her throat.

"Don't try to talk. You sustained serious damage to your throat, including your vocal chords. We're treating the injury, and you've responded well, but you won't be able to talk until the swelling of your larynx subsides considerably."

She closed her eyes as scattered images raced through her mind. *Pinned to the floor. The bulky man straddling her, putting all his weight on her abdomen. His hands around her neck. Squeezing. Not enough oxygen! Can't breathe! Tighter. Tighter.*

She sucked in air and reached for her neck, but her arms wouldn't lift her hands. Red, hot arrows of pain shot from her shoulders down to her wrists. *Oh, God!* She opened her eyes wide and looked into her lap. Everything was in clear focus.

Sophia reclined in a hospital bed, the standard white sheet pulled up to her chest. Her arms sat on top of the sheet. Her hands were wrapped in gauze, big as footballs. Her right arm was in a cast up above her elbow.

The skinny man holding a knife to Mamochka's *throat. Yelling. Demanding. The bulky one stepping on her right hand with his heavy, big boot. More pressure. The pain! Stop! Harder. Bones snapped. Please, please stop. The sobbing. Hers.* Mamochka's.

The pounding of her heart echoed in her head, shoving aside the beeping sound getting faster and louder. *No, Lord. Please!*

"Calm down, Ms. Montgomery. Your blood pressure is too high. I don't want to have to give you anything right now," the doctor said.

"You must relax now, *MIlaya Moyna*," the older lady whispered as she patted Sophia's head with the cool cloth again. There was something so familiar about her . . . but . . . not.

"There you go," Dr. Rhoads said. "Breathe slowly. In through your nose and out through your mouth."

Even breathing hurt, but Sophia controlled her panic. Years of practicing self-control had made her a master despite her fears. Her hands. How would she compete?

"Well done, Ms. Montgomery. I'll go over your injuries with you in detail, if you're ready." Dr. Rhoads stared at her, a single brow raised.

She nodded, sending slicing pain shooting down her spine. Sophia set her jaw and refused to wince.

"Okay." The doctor reviewed her chart. "You have sustained a laryngeal fracture with some mucosal tearing. We're keeping you on voice rest to minimize edema, hematoma formation, and subcutaneous emphysema. We will continue the use of humidified air to reduce crust formation and transient ciliary dysfunction. We'll also continue treatment by use of systemic corticosteroids to retard inflammation, swelling, and fibrosis and to help prevent granulation tissue formation."

Tears threatened, but Sophia blinked them back and concentrated on what the doctor said.

"Since you sustained compound fractures of the larynx, we have you on systemic antibiotics to reduce the high risk of local infection and perichondritis, which may delay healing and promote airway stenosis. You're also taking antireflux medications to reduce granulation tissue formation and tracheal stenosis." Dr. Rhoads smiled. "Of course, this means you can't eat or drink anything for a few more days. Understand so far?"

Sophia swallowed instinctively and regretted it immediately. She didn't understand everything the good doctor said, but she got enough to know her throat was damaged enough that she couldn't talk or eat. Still, it didn't sound permanent, so it was something.

He leaned forward, letting his weight add strength to his hands closed around her throat. No! She couldn't see past his face anymore. His scowl. His eyes. They weren't filled with rage, but just . . . empty.

"Sophia? Do you understand?" Dr. Rhoads asked.

She ignored the scattered images and gave a little nod. Her head began to throb in cadence with her heartbeat.

"Good. Moving on . . . you've sustained serious, traumatic crush injuries to both of your hands. In surgery, we were able to remove all the tissue we couldn't salvage. We were able to repair most of the damaged blood vessels to reestablish circulation in your fingers. All the broken bones were realigned and stabilized with temporary pins called K-wires and screws. We repaired the damaged tendons and ligaments. Post-op, you're doing great. You should be able to begin physical therapy as soon as the bandages are off." Again, the doctor smiled.

"Tell us." He stepped down on her hand. Pain. Bones cracked. Sophia cried out. "Stop!" Mamochka screamed. "Tell us." He put all his weight on his foot. Bounced. Sophia screamed and tried to roll over to protect her hand. He slung her backward and plopped onto her hips, straddling her.

The image disappeared. She stared at her hands lying gauzed and lifeless in her lap. Everything within her wanted to scream . . . cry . . . hit something. Why was this doctor smiling? Didn't he get it? Her hands were her life! If she couldn't sustain her weight on her hands, her career was over. *Dear Lord, no. Anything but this.*

"О'кей *MIlaya Moyna*," the woman whispered.

No, it wasn't okay. And who was this woman to be calling Sophia *my sweet*? Especially in Russian.

Despite the excruciating pain the movement caused, she twisted her head to meet the woman's stare. Sophia was certain she'd never met the woman before, but there was something . . . her eyes. They were just like *Mamochka's*.

Could it be? The woman looked to be about the right age.

"Now," Dr. Rhoads interrupted her thoughts, "about your pelvic girdle fracture."

Her pelvis was busted, too? *He straddled her. Mamochka yelled out. Sophia kicked, trying to buck him off of her. She had to help her mother! He pinned her with his weight. Pain shot through her mid-section and hips as if she'd missed a dismount and fell off the balance beam. "You aren't going anywhere. Ever," he whispered as he leaned over her and wrapped his hands around her neck.*

Unaware of her agony, the doctor continued. "There's only one breaking point along the pelvic ring, with limited disruption to the pelvic bone and no internal or external bleeding. This means your pelvis is still secure despite the injury, and we can expect a prognosis of a quick, successful and complete recovery."

Great. So her pelvis would have a complete recovery. She could live without being able to talk. But would her hands totally recover? If so, when?

She closed her eyes, refusing the tears access. All her life, coaches and instructors had drilled into her head crying was not an option. Tears were to be saved for her pillow.

So many before her had sustained injuries and left the circuit, only to never return. Was it her fate? *Abba!*

"The rest of your injuries are minor cuts and bruises that should heal without incident. Several areas required stitches. You have a laceration at the back of your head where you were hit from behind—"

"Doctor," a man's deep voice cut off Dr. Rhoads.

Even though things were a little fuzzy to Sophia right now, even she didn't miss the frown etched into the doctor's brow.

Dr. Rhoads smiled at her. "Ms. Montgomery, you were very lucky. With the extent of your injuries, you could have been in a coma."

The other man cleared his throat.

The doctor frowned as he looked at her. "Now, if you feel up to it, there's a detective here who would like to ask you a few questions. Only if you feel up to it. Do you?"

A detective? She swallowed, then regretted it, but still nodded.

The doctor nodded and stepped back. "Keep it brief, please, Detective. She needs her rest." Dr. Rhoads patted the bed beside her feet. "I'll be back later to check on you."

"Ms. Montgomery, I'm Detective Frazier." There was the deep voice again, authoritative, but with a hint of danger.

Sophia stared at him as he stepped into her line of vision, and took a full inventory of her first impression of him. Hard to gauge his height since she was in the bed, but he stood taller than Dr. Rhoads. Even though it was short, his black hair held a wave. He had broad shoulders and muscular arms apparent under the short-sleeve, button-down Oxford shirt he wore. He was probably no more than twenty-eight or so, at least in her estimation based upon the weariness in his face covered in stubble. His chin was cut and his cheekbones well defined. His nose had been broken at least once. But it was his eyes drawing her attention. They were so dark they appeared like a bar of dark chocolate.

Then again, maybe it was just her distorted vision.

⸻

Detective Julian Frazier had been silently assessing Sophia Montgomery from the corner of her hospital room since she'd been brought here following her surgery. Over the last two and a half hours, he'd gotten over the shock of her appearance. He'd been a cop for enough years that the damage a victim sustained shouldn't have affected him, but he'd seen the pictures of Sophia Montgomery before the assault and to see her now . . .

He pushed off the wall he'd been leaning against and approached her bedside. "I have a few questions. Do you know who you are?"

She nodded, and unless he was imagining things, she actually rolled her eyes.

Attitude. Good. She'd need it. According to the doctors, she had a long, painful road to recovery in front of her. "Do you know where you are?"

She stared at him from her swollen, cut, and bruised face. There wasn't one square inch of her face and neck without some visible sign of her assault. Even her lips were cut and cracked as she tried to lick them. With her head resting on the pillow, she gave a nod.

"Do you know why you're here?" he asked, flexing and unflexing his fingers against the coolness of the hospital room. It might be June outside, but the nurses had set the thermostat low enough it felt like winter in the critical care ward.

She blinked.

Then again.

He met her stare with his own. Something about how small she was and the damage inflicted on her, yet that she'd survived, nearly undid him. He'd overheard the nurses talking. They'd seen more people struck by vehicles with less damage than Sophia had endured. Whoever had attacked Sophia Montgomery and her mother had been especially vicious. Julian couldn't stand it. Whoever was responsible would face justice.

"Do you know why you're here?" he asked her again.

She tilted her head to the side. With her injuries, it had to hurt.

"You're unsure?"

She nodded.

Great. If she didn't remember anything, it would make his job so much more difficult. As it was, he was at a loss as to how he'd proceed at this point. With her extensive injuries, she couldn't speak and couldn't write, so how he was supposed to get her statement was more than a little confusing. He'd definitely have to think outside the box on this one.

She mouthed something. He couldn't tell what. She mouthed it again. It was one syllable, but he couldn't make it out. She mouthed it a third time.

"I'm sorry, but I don't understand." He snapped his fingers. "Let me get someone to help, okay?"

She nodded, but not before she shot him a look of pure frustration.

He could relate. Ever since he'd been called to the crime scene at almost eleven last night, frustration had been his constant companion. Frustrated this had happened. Frustrated no one had gotten there in time. Frustrated there were no immediate suspects.

Julian turned and stepped out of the hospital room, grabbing his cell phone from his hip. He quickly called his partner.

"She awake?" Brody Alexander asked without greeting. His partner was not one to waste time or breath with small talk when there was work to be done.

"Yep. Listen, we need to get Charlie up here ASAP to read her lips, so I can take her statement." Julian stared over his shoulder at Sophia's small and broken form lying so helplessly in the hospital bed. "And send some uniforms. I want someone posted by her room twenty-four-seven until we know what's going on."

"Got it." Brody hung up, business concluded. He might have an abrupt personality that had earned his reputation as an unappealing partner, but he suited Julian. After what happened with Eli, he wanted someone like Brody Alexander: all business.

He needed someone like Brody.

Julian put his cell back in its belt clip, strode back into the hospital room, and observed. It had taken the police some time to locate Alena Borin as Sophia's next of kin, only finding the connection through Sophia's mother's maiden name. The older woman fussed over Sophia, but Sophia didn't look like she recognized her grandmother. Maybe she had suffered some sort of brain injury in the attack. It would make his job much more difficult.

But not impossible. Because Julian refused to let whoever was behind this go unpunished. Someone would pay for this violence. He owed it to Sophia and her mother. The image of Sophia at the crime scene was one he would never forget. It would probably haunt him forever.

He returned to Sophia's bedside. Her eyes were guarded as she watched Alena Borin's every move: straightening the covers, gently bathing her forehead with the damp cloth. Sophia shifted her focus to collide with his gaze.

The uncertainty in her stare tugged at something buried deep within him. Something he didn't want to pull out and inspect. He cleared his throat until Ms. Borin gave him her attention.

"I've called in a lip reader to take Ms. Montgomery's statement," he said to her privately, in a low enough voice Sophia couldn't hear him. "This will take some time, and I'm sorry, but you can't be present. Why don't you go have some lunch?"

The older lady scowled at him, shaking her head.

"Ma'am, you don't have a choice. This is official police business."

She glanced down at Sophia, then back to him. "I will not leave her alone."

"She won't be alone. I'll be here the entire time, and there will be officers outside her door within the hour."

A long moment passed. She didn't say anything, nor did she move.

"Ma'am . . ."

Ms. Borin snatched up her purse. She smiled at Sophia. "I will be back in less than an hour, *MIlaya Moyna*." After patting the foot of the bed and throwing Julian another glare, she marched out of the hospital room.

Julian pulled the chair closer to the bed and sat. Sophia stared at him from behind her swollen face. He could read the wariness in her eyes as if it were a blazing neon sign.

"Do you know who that woman was?" He made a deliberate effort to speak just above a whisper level. The nurses had mentioned she'd probably have a horrible headache when she woke.

She shook her head—no, tilted it.

"You don't recognize her?"

She tilted her head again.

"You aren't sure who she is?"

A nod.

Julian stopped. Maybe he should wait for the lip reader, so he didn't misunderstand. She wasn't sure if she recognized and knew who Alena Borin was.

Sophia made a sound, but the pain it caused her marched across her face. She mouthed a single word, and this time, Julian understood exactly. "Who is she?" he asked.

She nodded.

He sat up straighter and looked her dead in the eye. "She's Alena Borin, your grandmother."

2

Her grandmother?

Sophia shook her head until the shooting pain reminded her of her condition.

"You don't recognize your own grandmother?" the handsome detective asked.

Well . . . her eyes *did* look like *Mamochka's*, and she would be about the right age. It was possible . . . but, no. *Mamochka's* mother had died years ago. That's what her mother had told Sophia all her life.

But she had spoken in Russian, with a similar accent to *Mamochka's*.

Had her mother lied all this time? Sure, Sophia knew the story of why her mother and grandmother were estranged, but *Mamochka* had said she'd died before Sophia was even born. Was it possible?

If it was, why had her mother lied to her all these years?

"I don't mean to distress you, Ms. Montgomery," Detective Frazier said. He smiled, and Sophia considered he probably didn't do it enough. Not with those deep, frown lines etched between his eyebrows.

Sophia could read his expression easily enough: if she didn't recognize her own grandmother, she must have more injuries than the doctor had addressed. There was no way he could know Sophia had been told her entire life that her grandmother was dead.

A twenty-something woman with long, auburn hair walked into the room. Detective Frazier turned, shook her hand, and they spoke in whispers. Sophia hated that. They were talking about her, but just like the nurses who came in during the night and spoke to the older lady—her grandmother?—they would do so in whispers so Sophia couldn't make out their words. Why wouldn't they tell her everything instead of everybody else?

Was she so bad off? Mercy, was she going to *die*?

"Ms. Montgomery," Detective Frazier interrupted her morbid thoughts. "This is Charlie Wallace. I asked her to come by and help us out since she can read lips, and I need to take your statement. Do you understand?"

Seriously? She looked at Charlie Wallace and mouthed, "Does he think I'm so stupid I can't understand English? It is my first language, after all."

Charlie laughed.

"What?" Detective Frazier asked.

"She's insulted you're talking to her like she's stupid and can't understand English. She's reminding you it's her first language."

The detective smiled. "Well, at least you haven't lost your sensibilities. I apologize for insulting you." He pulled up a chair and sat beside her bed. "I need to take your statement. If you could just answer the questions, Charlie will tell me," he turned to stare at the beautiful young redhead, "verbatim what you said." He smiled at Sophia. "Okay?"

Charlie moved to stand behind the detective. "Just speak to Julian like you're having a regular conversation. Don't try to enunciate your words. Just mouth naturally and I should be able to read you. If I miss something, move something to get my attention and we can back up. Okay?"

"Fine."

"She's good to go," Charlie told the detective.

"Great." Julian Frazier opened his notebook and sat it on his lap. He tapped his pen against the pad. "Do you remember what happened to put you in the hospital?"

The banging. "Someone knocked at the door. I was expecting a delivery from my coach, and we knew it would be late in the evening before the package would arrive. My mother answered the door." She paused as Charlie said the words almost with her. "Where's my mother?" She hadn't heard a thing about *Mamochka.* Was her mother in another room here at the hospital?

Julian nodded. "We'll get to her in a few minutes. Please, I need to know what happened."

Maybe they needed to compare her and *Mamochka's* statements. She took a deep breath and continued mouthing. "It wasn't my delivery. It was two men. They charged my mother, pushing into the house. They had big knives. They shoved *Mamochka* across the room. I ran to help." It was odd to hear her words coming out of Charlie's mouth.

"Sophia, I don't understand what they shoved across the room. I couldn't make it out," Charlie said.

She shook her head. "Not what. Who. My mother. It's Russian for mother. *Mamochka.*"

"Ah. MAM-och-ka?"

She nodded.

Charlie turned to Julian. "They shoved her mother across the room. She calls her mother by the Russian term for mother. *Mamochka.*"

Julian nodded. "Do you have any idea about what time this was?"

"A little after eight. We'd been waiting for the papers my coach had overnighted."

"Please. Continue."

Sophia closed her eyes and summoned the memories.

"One of the men grabbed me by the hair and threw me down. I think I hit my head against the leg of the old chair." She'd tasted the sharp tang of blood.

"Did you recognize the men?" Julian asked.

She shook her head, then remembered her injuries. "No. But they spoke a lot of Russian. *Mamochka* spoke to them. I don't speak fluent Russian, but I know enough. She was begging them to leave me out of it."

"Out of it? Out of what?"

"I don't know." She locked stares with the detective. If only she knew. "You'll have to ask my mother."

"Let's continue, shall we?" Julian shifted and made notes in his notebook. "Did you recognize the men?"

She shook her head.

"Can you describe them?"

She closed her eyes again. Their stench filled her nostrils. "They stank, like they hadn't showered in days. At least, the bulky man did. He was the one closest to me." She tightened her pinched-shut eyes, willing forth the images she'd banished. "Maybe a little under six feet. Bulky with muscles, not fat. Like he worked out." She opened her eyes to look at the detective, who wrote down the words Charlie spoke aloud. "Built like you, but his shoulders were a little wider."

Julian Frazier stopped writing and stared at her. Something about his look made her want to squirm, but the pain prevented her. After a long beat, he jotted something in his notebook.

Sophia swallowed, the pain radiating from her throat brought tears to her eyes. No, she'd push through this. "The other man was skinnier. And shorter. Probably about five-five or so." She struggled to recall details. Nothing came to mind. "I'm sorry. I don't remember much about him."

"Do you recall either's hair color?" Julian asked.

"The bulky man's head was shaved." She concentrated on the fuzzy images.

"What about the other man?"

She remembered the man putting a knife at her mother's throat. "Dirty blond, I think. It's hard to remember. He wore a black *ushanka*."

"A what?" Julian asked, turning to Charlie as if she'd mispronounced it on purpose.

Sophia tried to smile, but it hurt her face. "A Russian winter hat. Furry. Ear flaps."

"Ah. I got you." He scribbled in his notebook again. "Okay. So, after they barged in, what happened?"

"The skinny man . . . he had a knife. He yelled at my mother. Kept asking where it was." The scattered memories scraped against her heart. *Mamochka* had been so scared. Her eyes wide and her face ashen.

"What was he looking for?" Julian asked, snatching Sophia back to the present.

She opened her eyes and stared at him. "I don't know. *Mamochka* talked to him in Russian so fast, I couldn't understand her. Or him." Tears threatened to spill, but Sophia blinked them away. "I could only make out bits and pieces of their conversation. The bulky man . . ." *His hands tightened around her throat. No air! Tighter. Tighter. She couldn't breathe. Tighter. Mamochka yelled at him to stop. Sophia kicked and bucked. His grip tightened even more. She couldn't even scream.*

"The bulky man what?" Julian asked.

Tears burned her eyes, but there was no blinking them away this time. "He choked me. Sat on my stomach, put both his hands around my neck, and squeezed. I kicked and struggled, but it didn't help. He kept choking me." Sobs rose from her chest, nearly strangling her as they exploded from her.

Only the echoes of her crying filled the hospital room. She didn't want to cry, especially not in front of these people, these strangers. Tears should be saved for her pillow, and she wanted to stop them from falling, desperately, but she couldn't. She could only yell out in silence, trapped. It was as if everything pent up inside her had been released. Her whole body shook . . . trembling as if she was back in the house . . . back in the moment of the attack.

"I'm sorry, Sophia. I can only imagine how difficult this must be for you." Julian's soft tone jerked her tears away.

Her lifelong training called for her to use people's pity as motivation to push away the pain and soldier on. She steadied her breathing. "I guess I passed out for a bit, because I don't remember him stopping." Sophia steeled herself, concentrating with her eyes clenched shut.

The knife to Mamochka's *throat. "Where is it?"* Mamochka *shaking her head. The knife sliced a sliver into the smooth skin of her neck. A thin line of blood shocked against her paleness.*

"They wanted something. They kept asking my mother where it was. She wouldn't tell them."

"Tell us where it is, or your daughter will never use her hands again." The bulky man stepped down on her hand in heavy, unforgiving boots. Pain. Bones cracked. Sophia cried out.

"Stop!" Mamochka *screamed.*

"Tell us."

"At first, she wouldn't tell them. They used me to try and make her tell them. They crushed my hands on purpose." Sophia stared at her throbbing, gauze-covered hands. He was right—she'd never be able to use her hands again. Not as a gymnast. The tears threatened again, but she pushed them away, refusing the weakness.

"What did they want?" Julian asked.

"I—" Sophia concentrated as hard as she could. "I don't know. My mother spoke Russian to them." She shook her head, trying to recall everything, but the scattered images all jumbled together.

He put all his weight on his foot crushing her hand. He bounced until bones cracked loudly. Sophia screamed and tried to roll over to protect her hand. He slung her backward and plopped onto her hips, straddling her. She kicked, trying to buck him off of her. He pinned her, bearing down on her. "You aren't going anywhere. Ever," he whispered as he leaned over her and wrapped his hands around her neck.

His hands around her neck. Squeezing. Not enough oxygen! She couldn't breathe! Tighter. Tighter.

Then everything went black.

"He crushed my hands to make my mother tell him where she'd hidden whatever it was he wanted. I don't know what it was—they were talking too fast in Russian. *Mamochka* yelled at him. He pinned me to the floor and choked me." Her heart pounded. "I don't remember anything else until I woke up here. In the hospital."

Julian nodded. "Thank you, Sophia. I know this is difficult."

"My mother? How is she? Is she here, too?" *Lord, please let her be better off than I am.*

Julian Frazier stared at her, his face whitening by the minute.

"Detective?" she mouthed.

Charlie tapped Julian's shoulder. "She's asking about her mother."

Julian closed his notebook. "Sophia, I'm sorry. Your mother didn't survive the attack."

Every bit of . . . everything just left Sophia entirely. She couldn't even cry. Her mind wouldn't process the news. *Mamochka . . .* dead? It wasn't even conceivable.

No, it couldn't be possible. There had to be a mistake. Her mother had to be alive.

God, please! Don't let her be dead. I need her.

But the look on Detective Julian Frazier's face was clear there was no mistake. Her mother was dead.

⚭

Julian clenched his hands into fists. Beat up, broken bones . . . Sophia Montgomery looked like a discarded doll. And now, he'd had to rip out the only bright light left in her life. He knew it was all part of the job, but this time . . . well, this time, it stung.

"I'm so sorry, Sophia." The apology sounded lame to his own ears.

She looked like a stone statue, wrapped in gauze in places and looking like she'd gone twelve rounds with the heavyweight champion. That she was even alive was a miracle and able to communicate was beyond belief.

"*Politsiya?*"

Julian faced Alena Borin, Sophia's grandmother who she didn't recognize. He needed to remember she'd lost her daughter on top of nearly losing her granddaughter. Sophia's road to recovery would be long and trying. He put on what he'd perfected as his reassuring smile and held up one finger. "Just one more moment, please."

He turned back to Sophia. "Your grandmother is back. Do you recognize her now?" Maybe she'd just been confused. Some of the pain medications she took could make anybody loopy. Add to that the trauma she'd endured, and a recipe for blocking things had been built.

She mouthed at Charlie, who repeated what she said. "I don't know her. My mother told me her mother had died before I was born. But . . . looking at her, I can see a resemblance to my mother. I just don't understand why *Mamochka* lied to me."

Julian paused, letting Charlie's voice fade away. What was he supposed to do?

"Would you like me to speak for you? With her, I mean?" Charlie asked.

Sophia hesitated. Julian couldn't quite read the emotions in her eyes, and he didn't think her injuries were what masked her feelings. Finally, she nodded. Julian waved Alena over. "Ms. Borin, this is Charlie Wallace. She's a lip reader and has been assisting Sophia with giving her statement." He paused, watching Sophia from the corner of his eye. By the slow rise and fall of her chest, it was apparent she was working up her courage. Or maybe she was trying to figure out what to say.

Her lips moved and Charlie spoke. "Who are you?"

Julian took in Alena's slight step backward, as if she'd been gently shoved. It was only for a moment, then she squared her shoulders. "*MIlaya Moyna*, I am your grandmother. *Babushka*."

"My mother's mother?"

Alena nodded. "*Da*."

The two women stared at one another. Julian couldn't imagine what Sophia had to be feeling. On top of being attacked, she'd just learned she'd lost her mother. The mother who'd lied to her about the grandmother standing in front of her now.

"Why did *Mamochka* tell me you were dead?"

"Dead?" Shock buried itself in the harsh lines of Alena's face. "She told you I was dead?"

Sophia nodded. "She told me you died before I was born. When she was still pregnant with me."

Alena snorted. "She lied."

"Obviously. Again I ask you, why?"

"I do not know." Alena shrugged and looked over her shoulder. Julian didn't miss the deceptive body language.

Neither did Sophia. "I think you do."

Alena shook her head and looked past Sophia to the monitors with all the cords and wires attached to Sophia. The steady droning *beep beep beep* and the humming of the humidifier were the only sounds in the room.

"I think I'd like for you to leave." Charlie's smooth voice split the silence.

Alena shot her stare to Sophia. "*Ne, MIlaya Moyna.* Do not send me away."

"Then tell me why *Mamochka* lied about you being dead." Sophia frowned. "And stop calling me that. I'm not your sweet."

Julian cocked a brow at Charlie, who gave an answering single-shoulder shrug.

"I think my Nina and me had a misunderstanding. It is why she lied to you about me being dead." Alena gripped the bed's bar with both hands. Her gnarled knuckles whitened.

"What kind of misunderstanding would make *Mamochka* so upset with her own mother that she'd tell me you were dead?"

Alena looked at Julian, then at Charlie, then finally back at Sophia. "Now is not good time to discuss."

"*Mamochka* is dead. There isn't a better time for you to tell me why she let me believe all my life you were dead. What did you do to her?" Charlie spoke without inflection, but the pain and anger behind Sophia's words were clear. Tears seeped from her swollen eyes and trickled down her cut and battered face.

Alena shook her head. "Oh, *MIlaya Moyna,* we should grieve together. It is not good to be so sad all alone."

"I told you to stop calling me that." Sophia shook her head. "I want you to go. Now."

The machine closest to the bed began to beep a little faster.

"Sophia, I do not want to upset you."

She wouldn't look at Alena. "Just go."

Dr. Rhoads rushed into the room. "That's enough questioning. My patient needs her rest." A nurse trailed him, a syringe in her hand. She shot the contents into Sophia's IV.

"Everyone out, please," the nurse said while the doctor reviewed the machine's printouts.

"I come back tomorrow. Maybe be better time for you." Alena blew Sophia a kiss.

Sophia's lips moved, but Charlie didn't speak. She mouthed at her again, faster this time.

"Because I don't want to tell her something you might regret later," Charlie told her.

"You need to leave now." No mistaking the emphasis from the good doctor.

Julian nodded, then met Sophia's eye. "Thank you. We'll come by tomorrow and give you an update. Don't worry about anything. I have officers stationed outside your room."

She nodded, but a little slower than she'd been responding. Whatever they'd given her was already taking effect.

Julian led Charlie into the hall. "I don't want her room left unguarded. Period," he told the uniformed officer sitting just outside the door. "This wasn't a random act of violence. This was directed at the young woman in there and her mother. They were looking for something specific, and I have no way of knowing yet if they got it. If they didn't, chances are they'll come back to her to find it. No one is allowed inside without my express permission except medical personnel, me, and my partner. Understood?"

The officer nodded. "Yes, sir."

Julian and Charlie walked to the elevator together. "She's a strong one," Charlie volunteered. "One of the stronger ones I've seen, given her circumstances."

"Yes, she is." Julian had been impressed with her poise under such circumstances. It was hard to believe she was only twenty-one. He'd read her file while he'd waited for her to wake up following surgery. He hated to admit he'd been captivated by what he'd learned about her. She certainly hadn't lived a charmed life, not by any means, but the young woman had proven she was special.

"It's none of my business, it being your case and all, but Julian, I read your crime scene notes so I would be prepared before seeing her. Whoever attacked her thought they'd killed her along with her mother. They left her for dead." Charlie stepped off the elevator into the lobby of the Arkansas hospital.

"I know, and I know where you're going. If they find out she's still alive, they could come after her again. She saw them. She can recognize them." Julian strode to the automatic double doors. They whooshed open, blasting him and Charlie with the late June heat. "And that makes her a liability to them."

3

Sophia listened to the clanking of the empty lunch trays being reloaded onto the carts. She'd slept soundly, at least to the best of her recollection, although she suspected the medication they'd given her last night had been part sedative. It would explain her feeling of grogginess earlier this morning, but she felt much better now. The steady hum of the humidifier running had become strangely comforting.

"Good afternoon. I promised you I would get you cleaned up today, so here I am," the shift nurse, Katie, was younger, and chipper. Her constant monologue was strangely soothing to Sophia as she bustled about filling a plastic bin with water and opening a bed-bath supply pack.

"You'll feel so much better after you're cleaned up, I promise you." Katie laid a towel across Sophia's chest. "Those men doctors don't get how a lady can feel one hundred times better just after getting washed up. It's in our DNA, I think." She set the bin on the adjustable table and wet a washcloth.

"Now, I know you can't talk just yet, so I'm going to have to watch your expression to see if any of this is too uncomfortable for you. If something doesn't feel comfortable, just make a sour face and I'll stop, okay?" Katie's smile was as open as her personality.

Sophia nodded.

"Great." Katie daubed at Sophia's face with a lukewarm cloth. It felt . . . nice. Sophia closed her eyes and relaxed back against her pillows.

"See? I told you this would make you feel better." Katie continued bathing Sophia's face, rinsing the cloth every so often in the water bin. She bathed her face, her neck, and to her shoulders, then gently dabbed at her scalp. It was heavenly.

"Much better. Let me go change the water and I'll wash the bottom part of your hair with real shampoo."

Sophia opened her eyes just in time to see the water in the bin. Murky. Was she *that* filthy?

Water ran in the bathroom, mingling with Katie's humming. For the first time since she woke up, she wondered what she looked like.

Katie returned, still smiling and chattering. She washed Sophia's hair from the nape of her neck down, then conditioned it and combed it out. She finished giving Sophia a sponge bath and helped her into a clean gown, washed her feet and put lotion on them before covering them in a fresh pair of socks, then brushed Sophia's teeth. "There, you must feel all better. You look like you do."

She did feel better, but she was also tired from all the exertion. Who would have ever thought Sophia Montgomery, dubbed the Energizer Bunny for her enthusiasm in practice as well as in competition, would get worn out just from getting a bath and clean clothes?

"Your doctor will do rounds soon. I'm sure he'll be quite impressed with how much better you look," Katie rambled as she picked up the items from the bath.

Again, Sophia wondered just how bad she looked. She glanced around the room and didn't see a mirror anywhere. Was she *that* scary looking? Was her face all scarred up? The men had taken her mother and her career already. Had they left her yet another constant reminder of their hate? Of their rage?

Lord, help me! I don't think I can get through this. I feel like I have nothing left. Please, help me feel You around me.

"There." Katie straightened the covers over Sophia. "You get a little rest now. Getting all prettied up can wear a patient out. I'll see you later." Katie left, pulling the door almost closed behind her.

Sophia leaned back against the fresh pillows Katie had fluffed. Her mother used to fluff her pillows the same way every night when she'd tucked her in and they'd said prayers together. Sophia stared at the ceiling, fighting back the overwhelming grief strangling her as physically as the bulky man had. She needed something else to think about.

Sitting up straighter in the bed, she struggled to remember what *Mamochka* had said about her mother, Alena. Over the years, Sophia had stopped asking about her grandmother, because her mother said she'd died just a few weeks or so before Sophia had been born.

Sophia knew her mother and grandmother hadn't agreed on *Mamochka's* marriage to Sophia's father, but from what *Mamochka* told Sophia, her mother had come around after *Mamochka* had gotten pregnant with Sophia.

Although, now that she thought about it, Sophia couldn't recall seeing any photos of her grandmother in any of *Mamochka's* pregnancy albums. There were pictures of Nina and Lance Montgomery in various stages of the pregnancy: getting an ultrasound, decorating the nursery, setting up the crib . . . but there wasn't even a single shot of Nina's mother in all the photos. Not even in the pictures of the baby shower.

What was the real story? What was the truth?

Sophia turned as Detective Frazier and Charlie Wallace knocked on the door. "May we come in?" Julian asked.

She nodded, taking advantage of her alertness to check out the detective. Oh, he was as handsome as she'd remembered, but there were specific traits she'd missed yesterday. Like the way his jaw and chin were so well defined. The depth of his dark eyes. The cord of muscles bunched in his neck. The way he walked with an uneven gait, almost a ragged swagger.

Having a mother who'd owned a dance studio and had once been *the* prima ballerina of the Russian ballet, Sophia appreciated the way people moved. She liked grace and fluidity, but there was something to be said for a masculine posture. Especially one as distinct as Detective Julian Frazier's.

"How are you feeling today?" he asked as he moved beside her bed. Even his voice sounded deeper today.

"Better," she mouthed, and Charlie spoke. Sophia smiled at Charlie and mouthed, "Thank you, Charlie. It's nice to see you again."

"Nice to see you, too." Charlie grinned at her. "You look better."

"Oh, so it's not nice to see me?" Julian teased.

She smiled at him, happy she could make the facial gesture today without the sharp, shooting pain. Then again, maybe it was the drugs, too. "It's nice to see you as well, Detective," she mouthed.

Charlie didn't say anything.

Julian looked at her over his shoulder. "What'd she say?"

"Nice to see you, too, but nicer to see me."

She did not!

Julian laughed and turned back to Sophia. "Charlie's such a notorious liar. Don't worry, I don't believe you said it."

She smiled a little wider.

Julian cleared his throat and his face took on the familiar serious appearance. He held a folder as he pulled the chair closer to her bed. "I'm sorry to bother you, but to catch whoever did this, I need as much information as I can."

She nodded. She wanted nothing more than to see the men punished for what they'd done to *Mamochka* . . . to her.

"I need you to look at some photos from your mother's house, if you can. Just to see if you can make out if anything is missing."

"I'll try, but I don't live there. I'd only been visiting for a week before they . . . well, just before," she mouthed and Charlie spoke.

Julian flashed a reassuring smile. "It's okay. Maybe something will jump out at you. Okay?" He took a couple of eight-by-tens from the folder.

She nodded.

He held the first one up for her to see. It was a shot of the front entry area. Where the attack had started. Sophia sucked in air and closed her eyes, not prepared for her gut reaction to seeing the crime scene.

"It's okay. Take deep breaths. Just focus on the individual things you see in the picture. Is there something missing?" Julian's voice was smooth. Soothing.

She exhaled slowly and opened her eyes. The photo was of the front door and entry. In the picture, the front door was ajar, the nicks and scrapes from the men's forced entry visible. Sophia moved on to inspect the rest of the photograph. The entry table laid on its side, the once delicately intricate vase now shattered in pieces across the wood floor.

The two men charging into the room with knives. Mamochka sliding across the floor. Running to help, but not getting much traction on the slick floor. Being grabbed by the hair—the pain of my head jerking backward, then flying through the air into the living room. Landing. Hard. My head clunking against the stone fireplace edge. Shooting, stabbing pain going down my neck into my spine. Fear grabbing me in the gut.

"I didn't hit my head on the chair leg like I thought yesterday. I hit the fireplace." Something about hearing Charlie say her words aloud made them more powerful. More meaningful.

"It's okay." Julian held the photo. "Just concentrate on this one picture. Is there anything missing?"

She focused. "The table's turned over. The vase is broken. I can't remember anything else there."

"Good." Julian flipped to the next picture and held it up for her to see. "What about here?"

The picture was of the living room, taken from the angle of the entryway. The wide-angle view had captured the entire room.

Sophia let out a deep breath.

"Just take in it pieces. It's okay." Julian rested his elbow on the bed beside her as he held the photograph for her to study.

She nodded and concentrated. Maybe if she just broke it down, like Julian suggested, she'd be okay. She focused on just the left corner of the picture. The edge of the armoire holding extra blankets, then the open doorway into the dining room and kitchen.

The armoire still stood, probably too heavy for them to flip over easily, but the drawers were crushed on the floor beside the piece of furniture. Blankets and afghans were ripped and lying in ruin on the broken wood.

The artistic tapestry that had hung over the doorway into the dining room had been ripped from the wall and scattered over the floor. The little table just inside the dining room that held *Mamochka's* heirloom sterling tea service lay crumpled on the floor. Pieces of silver, bent and deformed, were strewn all over the floor. Several scuff and scrape marks pocked the beautifully polished wood floors.

"I can't tell if there are any pieces of the silver tea service missing, but I see several, so I don't think they were after the family heirlooms."

"Good. You're doing great."

She pressed on. The next part of the photo was the little wall between the doorway to the dining and kitchen area and the first floor-to-ceiling window. The flat screen television was smashed on the floor. A little painting that had hung over the television with the art light attached, a painting one of *Mamochka's* dance students painted for her years ago, was cut from the frame, sliced and lying in pieces on the floor.

The destruction . . . the violence. *"Where is it, Nina? We can make the pain stop." The skinny blond wearing the absurd ush-anka—absurd because it was June in Arkansas . . . put his knife to* Mamochka's *throat. "You're going to die anyway, but we can stop the suffering. For you. And her." He nodded at Sophia. She arched her back, trying to knock off the bulky man straddling her.*

"No?" The skinny man sighed, then nodded to the bulky man.

He got off Sophia, and she sucked in a deep breath, but before she could even think of how to move away from him, his heavy boot stomped on her right hand. The bones crushed as pain like Sophia had never felt before surged up her arm. She screamed and thrashed, but he only applied more pressure.

"Stop!" Mamochka *yelled.*

"Then tell us where it is. You control how much she suffers, Nina. Where is it?"

Sophia didn't realize she was crying until Julian softly wiped her cheeks with a tissue. "I'm so sorry, Sophia. If there was any other way to get this information, I'd do it so as to not bother you, but you're our only witness."

The gentleness in his tone almost made her cry harder. But she was tough. She had to be. Countless coaches had drilled it into her head. Only the toughest and most determined could win. And she was determined to see whoever did this to them punished.

Lord, help me be strong.

She sniffed and smiled at him. "It's okay. It's just remembering . . . not having my mother here . . . well—"

"I understand. And we appreciate you doing this. It helps the case more than you know."

She let out a huff. "Okay. I remember they kept asking my mother where something was. I don't think it was in these pictures if they were asking where it was. I mean, if it was visible in the room, they wouldn't have to ask where it was, right?"

Julian nodded. "Probably, but we need to be sure. And you might notice something else in the photos we don't even know could be a clue."

"Okay." She focused back on the photograph.

The curtains covering the floor-to-ceiling windows facing the backyard were ripped, frayed material remnants clutching to the rods. The long, thin tapestries on either side were ripped apart and lying on the floor.

The two couches in the center of the living room, in front of the fireplace, along with the coffee table and chair with ottoman, were broken, ripped, and wrecked in the photograph. The beautiful Oriental rug in the center of the room was cut up, and the crystal chandelier lay shattered on the floor.

Unnecessary destruction. Just plain evil.

Even the lamps that had sat on either side of the fireplace and the candelabras that had decorated the mantle were now crushed and ground into the wood floor. Grown men having a temper-tantrum. It's all this was. If— "They didn't find it."

Julian sat up straighter and leaned closer to her hospital bed. "You remember what they were looking for?"

She shook her head. "Look at the pictures. They'd already killed my mother and left me for dead. Surely, what they were looking for wasn't small and clear enough to be hidden in the chandelier or candelabras. They were enraged because they didn't find whatever it was, and that's why they destroyed everything."

Julian nodded. "I thought so, too, but we have to go through the evidence as best we can. We don't want to miss anything."

She nodded, her mind racing. *The bulky man leaned over her and wrapped his hands around her neck. The leather smooth against her skin. Squeezing. Not enough oxygen! She couldn't breathe! Tighter. Tighter. Then everything went black.*

Sophia snapped her eyes open. "He wore gloves. They both did. Black. Leather. Like driving gloves."

Julian nodded as he wrote in his notebook. "Good."

Disappointment fluttered inside her. "But it means there won't be any fingerprints."

"It's okay. Every little detail helps," Julian reassured her. "Even the minor things you think are of no importance. Especially those things." He held the picture back up for her to see. "Is there anything you notice? Anything at all?"

She stared at the picture as a whole. Nothing jumped out at her. Well, nothing other than the senseless violence. She shook her head. The mess would take quite some time to clean up.

Staggering grief washed over her as she realized she'd never see her mother again.

"Can you think of anything odd or out of place that happened recently? Unusual phone calls? Seeing strange people? Anything?"

Sophia silently snorted. "It'd just been announced I made the U.S. Olympic gymnast team. We were plagued with unusual calls—reporters wanting interviews, publicists wanting to schedule appearances and group photos . . . all kinds of crazy stuff. Even though I'd come to spend some time with *Mamochka*, they found our number and called. A lot."

"Yes. I can imagine." Julian glanced at Charlie, then back at her.

"What?"

"We've managed to keep the news of the incident out of the press for now, knowing you'd prefer to recover privately, but there are reporters snooping around."

Sophia could imagine the yellow crime scene tape across the front drive. She shuddered.

"We just locked the gate at the end of your mother's driveway and have an officer in an unmarked car guarding the house. To the outside observer, it could appear you were just taking precautions against the increased interest."

"Thank you." But it wouldn't be long until people figured out something was amiss.

She needed to call her coach. They would have to call in one of the alternates to practice with the team. But . . . she looked at Charlie and mouthed, "Can you get a message to my coach for me?"

Charlie nodded. "I'll be happy to."

"Happy to what?" Julian asked.

"Get a message to her coach."

Julian looked at Sophia and shook his head. "Let's hold off on that for now. At the moment, nobody knows what happened. No one knows you're here. You're safer this way."

It took her a minute, then her pulse spiked. "If they know I'm alive and know I can identify them, they'll come back to kill me." Pure terror clawed against her heart.

Julian set his hand on her forearm, ever-so-lightly. "I have officers outside your room around the clock with instructions that only medical staff and law enforcement are approved to enter. And your grandmother."

Relief sent warmth down to her toes. At least she was safe for the time being. But aside from that, she didn't want Alena. "You can remove her from the approved list."

"Sophia, are you sure you want to do that?" Charlie asked.

"Until she can stop lying to me, yes." Sophia mouthed.

Charlie sighed.

"I need to let my coach know as soon as I can. I'm supposed to report to the training center next week, and they need to notify one of the alternates as soon as they can. I can't leave the team hanging." It nearly killed her to hear Charlie say the words aloud.

Before Julian could reply, a knock sounded at the door, then the door swung open.

"So, how's our patient today?" Dr. Rhoads strolled into the room with his usual air of authority. He flipped the top page of the chart in his hand as he moved alongside her bed.

"Better, I think," Sophia mouthed and Charlie spoke.

Dr. Rhoads glanced up from his chart to look across Sophia at Charlie. "I see. Are you a doctor, ma'am?"

Charlie and Julian chuckled as Charlie explained, "It's what she said, not me. I'm just a lip reader who's translating for Sophia."

"Well. You can be useful." Dr. Rhoads met Sophia's stare. "Would you mind her staying during my exam of you so you can answer some specific questions?"

Julian stood. "I think that's my cue to leave." He tucked the photos back in his folder under his arm. "I'll be back later, if it's okay?"

His smile knocked her off balance, and suddenly, Sophia was happy the nurse had cleaned her up.

4

Go back through everything again, then. Find me something." Julian slammed the phone down and stared at the reports spread across his desk. With all the technology and testing, forensics should have been able to find something, at least one thing he could use as a lead.

Nothing. Not one single piece of evidence. Not a clue to who had killed Nina Montgomery and left Sophia for dead. Not one single shred of anything to lead him to their identity.

The stench of burnt coffee filled the station. Most everyone had already been to lunch and returned, but no one had remembered to make fresh coffee, thus, the stench. Still, it was familiar to Julian. It was home, despite how much he'd tried to deny the fact earlier in the year.

Phones rang and people talked—a background soundtrack to Julian's concentration.

He leaned back in his chair and twirled his keyring on his index finger as he glared at his case notes open on the computer monitor. What was he missing?

His partner was still out in the field, rattling the cages of the usual suspects to see if there was any word on the crime beat about this attack. Somebody had to know something.

"Frazier!" Captain Pittman hollered from his office.

Dropping the keyring to the desk, Julian stood and stormed into his boss's office. "Yes, sir?"

The captain looked up, his thirty-some-odd years on the force evident in the deeply etched lines wrinkling his face. "Shut the door."

Uh-oh. That usually meant trouble. Julian did, then took a seat in front of the captain's desk. "Yes, sir?"

"Where's Alexander?"

"Conducting field interviews, sir."

The captain harrumphed. "Where are you two on the Montgomery case?"

Nowhere. "The initial forensic report yielded us nothing. I've requested they review again. I've been working with Sophia Montgomery—have her statement and have reviewed the crime scene photos. Nothing yet, but I'm going back this evening to question her again."

No reaction at all from Captain Pittman. Julian refused to give in to the strong urge to fidget under the older man's scrutiny.

"Frazier, we've got word from higher ups . . . we need something on this case. The media will be all over this as soon as so much as a whisper gets out. Sophia Montgomery is a hometown girl made big. Just last week, there was a feature article on her in our local paper about her making the Olympic team." The captain tossed the newspaper across the desk to Julian. "The local reporters are clamoring to interview her before she goes back to Texas next week to start training. We've already got three reports from the uniforms at the crime scene of having to run off the press."

Just what he didn't need. "I understand, Captain."

"When news of the attack comes out, and it'll come out sooner rather than later, mark my words, then we need to have some lead . . . something to tell the public to squelch local panic and national interest."

"Yes, sir. I understand."

"Frazier, do you know where Stoneham, Massachusetts, is?"

"Um . . . no, sir." Was it important to the case? Had he missed something?

"It's Nancy Kerrigan's hometown. And do you remember how the press descended upon the little town after the attack on Nancy?"

Julian remembered the whole Nancy Kerrigan and Tonya Harding Olympic attack incident. He nodded.

"The same kind of media coverage is about to descend on Hot Springs Village, Detective, and when it does, I want us to have an answer for those questions the reporters will ask in regard to whether we have any leads in the case. Do I make myself clear?"

"Yes, sir." Julian stood. He was already motivated to get a break in the case because . . . well, if he was honest, he'd have to say because something about Sophia Montgomery tugged at the protectiveness trait locked inside him. Cases like hers were the reason he'd become a cop in the first place. He grabbed the paper with the article on Sophia. "May I keep this, sir?"

"Sure. Take whatever you need, but get some jump on the case."

"Yes, sir." Julian headed back to his desk. He slumped into his chair and glared at the blinking cursor over his case notes. Nothing. Absolutely nothing.

He grabbed the paper and stared at the picture of Sophia in the *Arkansas Gazette*. Even in black-and-white newsprint, she looked so much better than she did right now. In the picture, she wore one of the Olympic team warm-up suits. Her long, wavy hair was pulled high into a ponytail at the top of her head. But it was her expression that drew the reader—him, Julian—in closer.

Pure, unadulterated happiness radiated from her smile, from her eyes . . . she practically beamed with bliss.

For the first time in a long, long time, Julian yearned for what he saw in her face, for what he missed in his own life. He coveted the peace she portrayed.

How long had it been since he'd been truly at peace? He couldn't remember.

"None of our informants had any information about the attack," Brody's comments jerked Julian's attention back into focus. He plopped down behind the desk across from Julian, leaning his long frame back in the chair. Always so serious, Brody looked much older than thirty-five, only six years older than Julian. He might be aged beyond his years, but he was also usually wiser as well.

"Forensics came up empty, too. I have them reviewing everything again." Julian shook his head and opened the file to the crime scene photos. "Sophia remembered they wore gloves, but surely, with this much damage, they had to leave something. A fiber. A hair. A single drop of sweat to give us DNA."

Wait a minute . . . sweat.

Julian snatched the phone and called the head of the forensics unit. Julian cut off the man's greeting. "This is Detective Julian Frazier again. Go over Nina Montgomery's clothing again. This time, look for bodily fluids to test for DNA, especially in her top. I have reason to believe her attacker might well have sweated on her."

"We'll see what we can find."

"This is priority, per Captain Pittman."

"I'll call you as soon as we finish."

Julian hung up the phone, the first twinge of excitement building in his veins.

"He sweated on her?" Brody asked from across the desks.

"Sophia remembers the man who attacked her mother was wearing one of those winter Russian hats. Fuzzy, furry, whatever, with flaps. Whatever, but it's hot here. The day of the attack, it was in the high nineties." Julian lifted his keychain and began spinning it on his finger. He always seemed to think better with the habit he'd picked up right out of the academy. "If he's exerting even the slightest bit of effort, which we know he was to be threatening Nina, then there's a good chance he sweat during the attack. And if he was bending over Nina, like Sophia has described, he could've sweat on her."

Brody nodded. "Hey, at least it's something, right?"

"Better than nothing." Julian would take a long shot over a big fat zero any day. "And we need something pretty fast." He brought Brody up to speed on his conversation with Captain Pittman.

"Sounds like we're in the hot seat," Brody said as he accessed the case file on his computer. "Captain doesn't like to look unflattering in the press. Especially since rumor has it he'll be running for police commissioner next year."

"So you heard it, too?" Julian shook his head. Just when they got somebody in the captain's office who was more of an asset than just a placeholder on a political path, they either retired or got political aspirations themselves. "I'd hoped Pittman would stay in the chair longer."

"Yeah, me, too. But he'll be a good commissioner. At least better than the numbskull we have now."

"True that." Almost every person in uniform had a beef with the current police commissioner because he'd cut the force every chance he got, if it made him look more attractive in some way. Cut hours, makes the budget look better. It was even worse because he'd never gone through the ranks with the guys. He'd always been an outsider.

"These all your notes from Montgomery's interview today?" Brody asked, pointing at the computer screen.

Julian nodded. "I'm going back later to see if she can give me a list of people who might have had something against her mother."

"It's clear she had something someone wanted pretty badly."

47

"Yeah, but Sophia hasn't a clue what. She did figure out her life could be at risk."

"We'd better hurry."

Julian nodded again. Time was of the essence . . . for more than one reason.

"Maybe we should take another look at the house. This time, knowing they were looking for something, we can focus on the obscure. What do you think?" Brody asked.

They had nothing else. Julian shut off his monitor and stood. "It beats sitting around here doing nothing." He shoved the newspaper with Sophia's smiling face into the folder and snapped it shut, then tucked it under his arm. He always carried his case file when he visited the scene of the crime. Sometimes it helped him see something he'd missed before.

"Let's go." Brody led the way out the back to their unmarked car.

The afternoon sun burned hot and bright on the asphalt parking lot.

Julian slipped into the passenger seat. Brody always drove. He kept their assigned car as well. Julian always preferred his own Dodge. A sweet 1972 black Charger. He'd spent three years restoring it himself. Well, with Eli's help.

A lump lodged in the back of Julian's throat. Would the reaction ever go away?

"Heard a lot of people were starting to nose around the Montgomery property," Brody said, as he pulled the car onto the street.

Julian nodded. "Captain said there was activity. Hope the uniforms are being vigilant."

"Me, too." Brody pushed a little harder on the accelerator. "I even asked some of our informants to see what the word on the street is about anything with Russians."

"Are you thinking like organized-crime type Russian?" Julian stared out the window to the setting sun. "Yeah, the Russian mob exists in places like New York or Boston, but in Hot Springs Village, Arkansas?" He laughed. "I don't think so."

"You never know. Nina Montgomery was a star ballerina in the Russian ballet back in her day, right? And the guys who attacked them were Russian. So, hey, it's not a far stretch to consider."

Brody had a point. Julian just couldn't wrap his mind around any type of organized crime being in their sleepy town, best known for its sweeping landscapes, natural settings, and championship golf courses. Twenty-six thousand acres, the town had a population of approximately thirteen thousand people. Most people moved to the village, as everyone affectionately called the town, in retirement, or the homes built were second homes. Places to stay for long golfing weekends or blocks of the summer. Many of the homeowners rented out their homes on a weekly or monthly basis. Hardly a hopping crime metropolis. Most of the crimes in the village were against property: those vacant homes. In a busy year, they'd see no more than eighteen or so violent crimes.

Nothing like this case. The attack was the most violent Julian had worked in years. Maybe it was the viciousness that made this one tighten his gut.

Or maybe it was Sophia Montgomery.

Brody turned off the highway onto the road where Nina Montgomery lived. "Charlie told me about Alena Borin. She's very Russian."

"She is." And there was some reason Nina Montgomery had lied to her daughter about Alena being dead. "Let's order a background on her. Maybe we'll get lucky and hit a connection. There has to be something we're missing." Julian pulled out his phone and called in the background check order.

Brody pulled the car to the gate of Nina Montgomery's home. The marked police car's door opened and a uniformed officer stepped out. "You can't—oh, I'm sorry, sir. I didn't recognize your car with the glare." He moved toward the gate and unwound the chain holding it closed.

"No problem. Has there been a lot of activity today?" Julian rolled down his window and asked the uniformed man.

"A little more than usual. Mainly reporters. One even tried to bribe me . . . said she needed to get an exclusive of mother and daughter before Sophia left to go into training." He shook his head and opened the gate. "I'll give it to them, they're a determined bunch."

"Good work. Thanks." Brody eased the car through the gate and down the drive toward the house.

Approaching, one wouldn't believe the acts of senseless violence that had occurred here. The house sat off the road about two hundred feet, hidden by large oak trees bordering the winding drive. Small crepe myrtle bushes decorated the area with bursts of pink, purple, and white. The overwhelming sweetness of honeysuckle filled the air.

The house itself was pretty basic: brick and siding, about nineteen hundred square feet, with a chimney jutting a few yards off the roof. Black shutters stood open at the windows on the front of the house, but Julian knew the floor-to-ceiling windows in the back of the house had no adornments on the outside, nothing to mar the view into the wooded backyard.

Had the two men approached from the woods in the back? By the time the police arrived, the first responders and ambulances had already run over any other identifying tire tracks in the driveway.

Brody parked the car. Julian stepped out and leaned against the hood, taking in the setting.

"What are you thinking?"

Julian opened the case file and summarized the timeline he'd created. "The coroner puts the time of Nina's death between nine thirty and ten. The delivery driver made the 911 call at nine fifty-five."

Staring off into space, Julian let his mind meander through the facts. "Taking into account Sophia's statement that they broke in a little after eight, I'm going to theorize Nina died around nine forty-five." He stared at Brody. "They would need at least an hour to barge in and begin the assault. For Sophia to have lost consciousness once, come back, then lose it again . . . it couldn't have happened quickly." A ball in the pit of Julian's stomach formed.

"According to her doctor and the coroner, the damage inflicted took at least forty minutes."

Julian swallowed the acidic reaction on his tongue. Forty minutes. They'd been tortured, plain and simple. Merciless. Nina's throat had finally been slit. Thankfully, they must have thought when Sophia lost consciousness the second time, she was dead. They'd moved on to search and destroy the house.

Brody continued his assessment. "So they kill Nina Montgomery at nine forty-five, then they searched the house for whatever they were looking for, assuming they didn't get it from Nina."

"Sophia said her mother didn't tell them where it was *at first.* But once they started torturing Sophia, I think the implication is Nina started talking."

Brody took the case file and flipped through it. "Sophia blacked out, so we don't know for sure." He handed the file back to Julian. "What if she gave it up? What if that's why they slit her throat and left Sophia alone? They went and retrieved whatever it was, then left. They never checked back on Sophia, only assumed she was dead."

Julian stared into the darkening woods. "Then how'd the house get so destroyed? If they got what they were looking for, why destroy the house? Why take the time, or worse yet, possibly leave some evidence of their identity?"

"True."

"I'm guessing one of two theories. One, Nina told them where it was and they killed her, then went to retrieve whatever it was, only to discover she lied. They tore apart the house, but didn't find it."

Brody nodded. "Works. And your other theory?"

"Nina saw Sophia fall unconscious again, but she thought Sophia was dead, so she refused to tell them anything. In a rage for her not telling them, they sliced her throat, then checked the house."

Brody did a slow three-sixty in front of the house. "Both of those theories could work, so the timeline would be Nina Montgomery was killed at nine forty-five."

Julian opened the folder. "The 911 call came in from the delivery driver. He was delivering Sophia's paperwork from her coach at the Olympic training center, and he had to get a signature. He rang the bell and got no answer. He knocked, then the door opened, and he saw Nina lying on the floor. He called it in at nine fifty-five." He shut the folder and moved to where he could see around the side of the house. "If they were tearing apart the house to find whatever it was, and he interrupted them, why didn't they just kill him? They'd already killed two people, why not kill the driver and keep searching the house?"

Brody shrugged. "Maybe they realized if he didn't scan the package receipt immediately, it would signal a problem immediately."

"So . . . it makes me wonder, how did they approach and leave?"

"What do you mean?" Brody asked.

"If the driver interrupted them, and he reports he didn't see anybody moving, nor did he see any other vehicle in the drive aside from Nina's, then where was their vehicle? If they had driven and parked in the drive, the delivery driver would have seen their car when he interrupted them and they ran off. But he didn't. It doesn't make any sense."

Brody shook his head and climbed the stairs to the front door. "None of this makes sense, but I want to know what happened. Everything. Even the stuff that doesn't make sense. I want the full picture."

"Me, too." Julian followed his partner into Nina Montgomery's house. "Me, too."

5

I just want to talk to my granddaughter."

Sophia opened her eyes and looked at the door to her hospital room. The police officer had stopped Alena from entering.

"I'm sorry, ma'am, but the last notification I received was that you were not to be admitted per the patient's request."

Alena must have made a face, because he added. "I'm sorry."

"I must talk with her. I am ready to explain what happened."

"I'm not supposed to disturb her. She's supposed to be resting."

"I need to tell her what happened."

A long pause filled the air. Sophia wiggled her way until she was more reclining than lying down.

The policeman stepped into her room. "Ms. Montgomery, are you awake?" he whispered.

She nodded, waiting for him to get close enough to see her in the dim light of the wall lamp. She flashed him a smile.

"Um. Your grand—Ms. Alena Borin is outside and would like to talk to you for a moment. Is it okay?"

Without Charlie, Sophia had no way to communicate, but maybe it was for the best. Maybe it would be better if Alena could just stand there and tell her story. Sophia could always just shut her eyes and stop listening. Goodness knows the boredom of the afternoon had been enough to have Sophia climbing the walls. After the doctor's rounds, Charlie had left, leaving Sophia alone and in silence.

Any conversation was better than none. Sophia nodded at the policeman.

"Are you sure?" he asked.

She smiled, and nodded again.

"Okay. I'll let her know she can only stay for a few minutes though, okay?"

She nodded a third time.

The policeman spun and returned to his post. Sophia took a moment to pray for the truth.

And for her own understanding.

"*MIlaya Moyna*, I am so happy you will see me." Alena dropped her oversized purse on the floor, then pulled the chair up beside Sophia's bed. "I am so sorry I was not able to tell you these stories earlier. There were too many people listening."

Sophia gave a slow nod. Well, they were alone now.

Alena gripped the side of the bed rail. "Nina, your mother, meant everything to me. From the day she was born, I knew I would live for her." Moisture glistened in her eyes. "When she first learned to walk, she did not just walk. She *skol'zili* across the floor. Such grace, even for a baby."

Sophia struggled over the word, her mind going through the limited Russian her mother had spoken fluently, but only taught Sophia when pushed. Finally, she grasped it from the corners of her memory. *Skol'zili* translated to *glide*.

"Nina went from walking to dancing immediately. She was born with the *talant*. So gifted. So natural. Beautiful. Poised."

Sophia's heart raced. *Mamochka* had referred to Sophia's gymnastic ability at a young age as the *talant*.

"I got her best instructors. Enrolled her in Vaganova Ballet Academy in St. Petersburg, Russia. At four years old, they accepted her. Knew, like me, she was destined to dance."

Just like Sophia's destiny was to be a gymnast. Or, well, it had been. Grief curled its perverted fist into her chest, causing her breathing to hitch.

"My husband, Nina's own *otets*, he come to complain of the cost. Said Nina's dance lessons were too expensive. Demanded she go to closer academy." Alena's finely tweezed eyebrows crinkled into a frown. "No one had heard of the instructor. No major ballet company would take dancers from such a studio."

Sophia's own father had died soon after she'd been born. She had some early photographs with him holding her, beaming. She couldn't imagine he'd deny her anything. But her father had been American, where daughters were their daddy's little girls. Sophia again, as she had many times over the course of her life, regretted her father had died before she got to know him. All she had were the memories her mother had shared with her.

"He refused to pay, so I took Nina and left."

It shocked Sophia back to Alena's story. She'd left her husband because he'd refused to pay for *Mamochka's* expensive dance lessons? That was just crazy. There had to be some sort of mis—

"It was a choice I made for my Nina. She needed the best chance. To see her dance was like watching *bog* breathe life." Alena's voice took on a dreamy tone that matched the faraway look in her eyes.

Sophia had seen her mother teach ballet for years and had grown up watching her dance on stage in recitals and local productions. She'd been amazing, but Sophia had never heard someone compare her mother's dancing to God breathing life.

"I do everything to pay for her lessons. I quilted, selling them for high prices. They were good. I am good quilter. I cleaned the studio for extra lessons for Nina. I sewed costumes for the troupe. I went days without eating, so Nina could dance."

Sophia thought of her mother in a new light. Had she known of the sacrifices Alena had made for her? Had given up willingly so she could follow her dreams? The quilting . . . *Mamochka* had quilted. She'd taught Sophia. It was something they did together. Often.

Alena's admission made Sophia wonder. What sacrifices had *Mamochka* made for Sophia's gymnastics that she didn't know about? It didn't matter now since she would never be a gymnast again.

"Nina was beautiful ballerina. As she matured as a dancer, she get more and more beautiful. Everyone says she is perfection *en pointe*." Alena smiled, more to herself than at Sophia.

"She land the role of Little Radish in *Cipollino*. At eleven. Nobody ever dance Little Radish at eleven. The press fall in love with her. She looked like a princess and dance like a goddess. Everyone wanted her. Then, she get chance to attend Kirov Academy of Ballet. Finishing school there, the ballerinas can dance around the world, not just in Russia. It is great opportunity for my Nina, so I accept the offer and we move to United States." Alena's eyes widened then.

Sophia tried to imagine what it was like to sacrifice everything, even your own marriage, for your child's dreams. Then to move to a strange country where you didn't know anyone. She couldn't begin to fathom how scary and hard it must have been. She begrudgingly looked at Alena with a bit more respect.

"We get settled in home in Washington D.C. Nina dances and dances and dances. Her dreams coming true. She looks beautiful on stage. When she is only twelve, she become a prima ballerina as the Sea Princess in *The Little Humpbacked Horse*." The pride was obvious in Alena's voice. "Everyone loves my Nina. Her best friend, Nadia, is competition, but knows Nina is best dancer."

"After Nina graduates at seventeen from Kirov, she is welcomed to New York Ballet Company. Nadia goes with her, but not as principal dancer like Nina, but as *Corps de Ballet*. Nina's first performance after joining, she dances the title role in *Raymonda*, and people take notice of her dancing. How she is best they have ever seen. They compare her to such prima ballerinas as Natalia Bessmertnova and Galina Ulanova."

Sophia could see how. Her mother could dance. Sophia used to sit in the corner at the dance studio and watch *Mamochka* warm up before dance classes. Every movement she made was perfectly executed and in perfect time to the music.

"Nina prima ballerina in company performing in all the best productions. The biggest. She demands attention. Even from young men. I discourage most, but there is one who is fitting for her. Dimitri. From first day I meet him, I see Dimitri is in love with her. He is wealthy. He is ballet dancer, too, but not like Nina. Still, he will advance her career, so I try to keep the other young men away from her. She must concentrate on her dancing. Her career. I have given up everything for her success." Alena's voice wobbled a little.

Sophia could easily see how domineering Alena could be. Had *Mamochka* felt smothered? Or like she had missed out on a childhood? Sometimes, Sophia wondered if she'd done just the same thing herself. For as long as she could remember, she'd lived by a different set of rules. She'd eaten the healthiest of diets, all for strength and muscle building. While other girls in school were talking about the coolest fashions, Sophia got excited over her gym getting a new balance beam. When her teenage peers were getting ready for their first dance, Sophia was getting up at four in the morning to practice for three hours before showering and changing for school, then practicing for three or four more hours every afternoon.

It was a choice she'd made. Her mother hadn't pressured her, but *Mamochka* hadn't shown her another way of life, either.

Alena cleared her throat. "One of those boys was Lance. He was wrong for my Nina. He did not understand her dedication. Her determination. He could not appreciate her talent." She snorted. "He was not even a dancer or in the dance world. Not like Dimitri."

Her father. Sophia tilted her head.

"He sweep my Nina off her feet. I try to tell Nina to stay away from the American with the shiny eyes, but she not listen to me. He was a bad influence on her. I call Dimitri for help, to stop this romance, but it was too late. Nina disobeyed me. She snuck out to see him. This . . . this . . . *voyennyy* boy."

Sophia shook her head. She didn't recognize the Russian term. What kind of boy? She shook her head faster.

Alena paused, understood. She opened her mouth, then shut it. Then she tried again. "Service." She held up her hands and made a mock gun and shooting gesture. "Uniform."

Ah. Military. Her father had been in the Air Force. Sophia nodded.

"Nina think she love this Lance. I try to tell her it is not real love. It is only infatuation. I ask her to consider Dimitri, but she keep seeing her Lance, even when I forbade her to see him anymore."

Sophia smiled softly. As a child, she'd begged her mother to tell her the story of how she met her father. Over and over. *Mamochka* said it was love at first sight. She'd seen Sophia's father in the audience at a performance, looking handsome in his Air Force uniform, and her heart had danced to live in Lance Montgomery's hands. Sophia had always thought that was so utterly romantic.

"He would not go away, and Nina became more and more difficult. I hire her a new manager, who agrees with me this Lance needs to go. Dimitri comes to see her, tries to tell her he loves her, but understands Nina needs to concentrate on her dancing. With the new manager help, we move." Alena shook her head, staring off into space as if she'd forgotten where she was entirely. "Dimitri is devastated, his heart broken."

"We move, and not tell this boy where we move to. Nina was distraught, but she continued to dance. Nadia stays with Nina more and more, hoping to cheer up Nina. My Nina . . . her dancing becomes more emotional. More powerful. She put her sadness into her dance, and she could demand whatever she want for a performance."

Sophia's heart ached for the young woman her mother had been. In love, but taken away. She'd thrown her passion into her dancing. Sophia understood only too well. The one guy she'd liked, who she thought could've been the one, had been a disappointment and wanted to rush things between them. When she wouldn't be pushed, he dumped her. Afterward, Sophia had thrown herself into gymnastics with a renewed vengeance. She'd done some of her best uneven bars work after the breakup.

"But it was too late. A month later, Nina got so sick she threw up during a performance. She was rushed to the hospital, where they tell her she is pregnant."

Now this was news. *Mamochka* never mentioned she'd gotten pregnant before she was married. Forgetting her face was still swollen, Sophia frowned. The sharp pain reminded her.

"*Da, MIlaya Moyna,* she found out she was pregnant with you. I swore Nadia to secrecy and fired new manager."

Even if she could speak, Sophia wouldn't have been able to say anything. *Mamochka* had said she'd gotten pregnant almost immediately after getting married. To now find out she'd gotten pregnant before she was married . . .

"I am sorry to admit, but I told Nina to get rid of the baby. Having it would ruin her career and she would never dance again. Not as a prima ballerina." Alena's face turned red. "I am not proud to tell you this, but this is truth. This is what I said to my daughter."

Alena wanted *Mamochka* to . . . to . . . abort her? Sophia felt sick to her stomach, even though she hadn't had food to eat since she'd come into the hospital.

"Please understand, *MIlaya Moyna,* I had sacrificed everything for my Nina. So she could be the prima ballerina she was born to be. She had opportunities. We could go anywhere, do anything. She was just eighteen. Barely eighteen, and she had made a mistake. I am sorry, but she did."

Sophia shook her head, screaming in silence for Alena to stop! Just stop!

But Alena couldn't hear the cries. "I am sorry, but this is truth of how I felt. I see my Nina about to throw away her career, her life. I tell her this, but she refuse. She find this Lance and contacts him. He comes and takes my Nina away. To here."

Sophia couldn't believe what she was hearing. Her own grandmother wanted her aborted! It was inconceivable.

"I followed her to Arkansas. I beg her to listen to me. He wanted to marry her, but she still not legal age in Arkansas at that time, so they wanted me to sign form to let her marry him. I refuse. She swear she never speak to me again. I still refused. I still think maybe she do as I ask and save her career. I beg her to reconsider Dimitri if she need love so bad, but she not consider anything but marrying her Lance and throwing away her dancing."

Sophia didn't even try to stop the tears from forming in her eyes. She let their hotness scorch her eyelids. The pain reminded her that she was alive, no thanks to her *grandmother.*

"I thought she give in, if I refuse to sign papers. Think maybe she will change her mind once I refuse again. She was turning her back on every sacrifice I had made for her. For her dancing. For her to be best ballerina ever."

If it didn't hurt so bad, Sophia would have ground her teeth. As it was, she was finding it hard to understand how her mother ever forgave Alena, but *Mamochka* had said they'd reconciled before she was born.

Then again, she'd told Sophia that Alena had died.

"I did not think she would track down her father and get him to sign the form." Alena snorted again. "Stupid man. Signing just to get back at me for leaving him. He always hated Nina dancing."

How could Alena be so cold? So cruel?

"My Nina marry Lance. I cried on her wedding day, when she came to tell me. She wanted me to be happy. Said we could be family. Lance said I could even live with them." Alena's English got more broken the faster she talked.

"But I refuse. I tell Nina there is still time. She can still be dancer. She can get rid of pregnancy and get marriage annulled." Alena shook her head. "But she tell me no. Told me I would change my mind about my grandchild."

Everything inside Sophia felt cold, as if it was the dead of winter instead the beginning of summer. This woman . . . her grandmother . . . was colder than the iciest of polar vortexes.

"But I could not forgive her. Every time I looked at my Nina with her fat belly, I can only see her throw the sacrifices I made away. I gave my entire life for her dancing, and she throw it away for a man. Nadia soon replaced her as prima ballerina in New York City Ballet Company and in Dimitri's heart."

For a man and her baby. For Sophia. How could Alena not see the pain her words cut through Sophia? She probably didn't care. She certainly never had before.

Alena looked at Sophia. "I realize I was wrong after Lance died. I try to see Nina and you. I try to tell her I am so sorry. But she tells me she never want to see me again. That I am no longer her mother."

Sophia cried inside for her mother. Poor *Mamochka* . . . she was a new wife and mother and her husband had just been killed. She had to face her mother, the woman who had all but demanded she abort her baby. The woman who had tried to keep her from the man she loved. The woman who had abandoned her daughter because of her own dreams.

"I am sorry, Sophia." Alena's tears slipped down her cheeks. "If I could go back, I would do things different."

Would she? Or would she keep her own desires for Nina above what her daughter wanted most?

"I am your *Babushka*. I made mistake with Nina, but I am here for you. To take care of you."

Sophia closed her eyes and turned her head. It was too much for her to handle right now. She couldn't deal with Alena Borin.

It was probably a good thing Sophia couldn't speak because if she could, she would probably say a lot to her *grandmother* that wasn't found in the New Testament.

6

Thanks for agreeing to see us again, Sophia. I know it's late and you need your rest. I'll keep this as short as I can." Julian noticed that although the swelling had gone down even more in Sophia's face, her eyes held more of a haunting look than earlier.

She had, after all, just lost her mother. Grief would most likely be settling in. The reality always came sometime after the initial shock of losing a loved one. Each person was different.

"This is my partner, Brody Alexander."

Brody nodded. "We'll be brief."

"Anything to help solve my mother's murder." Charlie's voice was void of emotion, but Julian could feel the determination radiating from Sophia.

"Going back over your statement and the case notes, I have a few other questions." Julian opened his notebook, knowing Brody was doing the same from the other side of the room without even looking. They both liked taking their own notes, then entering them into the same case file they shared. Sometimes it helped trigger a new lead by having their different perspectives in black and white.

"Ask away."

Everything about Sophia seemed *off* at the moment. It unnerved Julian. He wasn't sure why he felt like he did—he certainly didn't usually feel this way about victims on cases he worked. He didn't like the sensations. Made him feel . . . well . . . made him *feel* and he'd managed to stop doing so for some time now. He didn't like remembering what emotions did to him.

Brody cleared his throat, snagging Julian's attention.

"Right." He looked up from the file and smiled at Sophia. "We're working on the timeline. Can you tell me what you were doing before the men knocked on the door?"

"*Mamochka* and I had a late dinner. We finished cleaning up the kitchen, then we had been sitting in the living room talking about my training. Coach Douglas had told me earlier he'd overnighted my training contract, and I should expect it on Thursday evening. We were waiting on the delivery while we talked."

Julian made a note. "Was the television on? Dishwasher running? Anything making a steady noise?"

"We had music on softly in the kitchen, as we usually did." Sophia tilted her head and stared hard at Julian. "Why?"

Even though Charlie spoke the words, the question reached Sophia's eyes.

Julian leaned forward. He had to proceed carefully with pulling out this information. "Do you remember hearing anything before the knock on the door?"

Sophia closed her eyes. Even with her injuries, twitches and tension conveyed her concentration.

Brody pushed off the opposite wall, holding his tablet handy. He preferred to write his notes on his electronic tablet, then have the document of his notes sent to the case file. Julian preferred the pen and paper. He just felt more connected with ink flowing from his pen or pencil.

Sophia opened her eyes. "There was an engine sound. Like a scooter or golf cart. Not loud, but like those types of engines hum."

"You didn't hear a vehicle in the drive? Could you have mistaken it for the delivery truck?" He shouldn't lead the witness in any part of giving a statement, but Julian needed to be sure. This was very important.

Sophia shook her head. "No, and now, in hindsight, I realize we probably shouldn't have just opened the door without checking. But we were expecting the delivery, so we just did."

"What about anything else you might remember? Any other sounds?" Julian pushed.

Again she closed her eyes for a moment, then opened them again. "No. I'm sorry. I don't remember hearing anything else."

Julian smiled and patted her covered leg. "No, you're doing great."

"Doesn't feel like it."

"You are."

Brody stepped forward. "Ms. Montgomery, about your—"

"Please, call me Sophia. When you say *Ms. Montgomery*, it sounds like you're addressing my mother, and . . ."

"I understand." Brody flashed her one of his rare smiles.

Julian pressed his lips together and stared at the file in his lap. She'd gotten to the hard-nosed Brody Alexander, too. There was definitely something special about Sophia Montgomery.

Brody continued. "Sophia, can you think of anyone your mother had problems with recently?"

"I'd only been here a week visiting. I live in Plano, Texas, so I don't know who my mother had problems with."

"Anything she might have mentioned? Something she told you on the phone recently, perhaps?" Brody asked.

Sophia shook her head and mouthed. "I was busy training for nationals, so my phone conversations with my mother were brief. After nationals, they announced the Olympic team members. We did the whole press thing, then had two weeks before we are supposed to report to the training center in Huntsville, Texas. I came home to visit *Mamochka*."

"Do you know if she kept a diary?" Julian asked.

"No—I-I'm not sure."

"Is it possible she did?"

"Maybe."

"Did your mother mention anything about having problems with anyone?" Julian asked.

"No, but apparently, my mother didn't tell me everything."

"Is there anyone you can think of who didn't like your mother or had a grudge against her?" Brody tapped his stylus against his chin.

"I'm not aware of anyone." Sophia frowned. "Well, aside from her mother, Alena Borin."

Julian and Brody made eye contact over the hospital bed. "Your grandmother?" Brody asked.

Sophia nodded. "She and my mother were estranged. My mother had lied to me all my life, telling me Alena was dead."

Yeah, he already knew that. Julian patted the covers over her leg again. "Have you talked with Alena since she left?"

She stared at Julian and slowly nodded. No denying the unshed tears she blinked away. "She came earlier. She wanted to explain. Told me the truth."

Julian locked stares with Brody again.

"Oh, your police officer was nice and came in and asked if it was okay before he let her in. I gave permission. Although now, I wish I hadn't."

An unfamiliar knot tightened in Julian's chest. "You think she had a grudge against your mother?"

"Oh, she did. No question about it." Sophia blinked rapidly.

Julian groaned inside. If she started crying again, it just might undo him.

"She begrudged my mother for daring to fall in love. Even worse, she held a grudge against my mother for giving up her dancing career to have a child. Apparently, she begged my mother to abort me, but my mother refused. Alena wouldn't forgive her. She's held a grudge ever since."

It took all of Julian's strength not to reach out and pull Sophia into his arms, and he couldn't even explain why. If there was ever someone needing compassion and protection, it was Sophia Montgomery. Maybe that's what made him feel so unusual. So out of character.

But he couldn't do that.

Brody cleared his throat. "Um, Sophia, do you think your— Alena could be involved somehow in the attack on you and your mother? Is that what you meant?"

Sophia paused for what seemed like several minutes, and for a moment, Julian wondered if her meds had kicked in and she'd dozed off. Finally, she mouthed.

"No. There's no logic to it," Charlie said for her. "I was trying to make the point there are people I'd least expect who have grudges or harbor ill feelings. My mother and her mother were estranged, yet all my life, my mother, who I thought was always honest and upfront with me, had lied to me. I would have never believed it if someone had told me, but here it is, the truth."

Sophia stared at Brody. "So, to answer your question, I know of no one who made threats against my mother, but that isn't saying much."

Her emotional agony was as clear in her statement as her physical injuries. Julian couldn't imagine how she felt. Her own grandmother had wanted her aborted—it had to cut right through her heart. Especially with someone as emotionally vulnerable, at the moment, as Sophia. Injuries aside, she'd lost her mother and the only career she'd ever known. Now to find out her own grandmother had despised her existence so much that she stopped talking to her daughter because of it . . . no wonder Sophia acted differently now. She had a lot to deal with all at once.

"Had your mother acted oddly during your visit? Maybe received a phone call and acted upset afterward?" Brody asked.

Sophia shook her head. "Not that I recall."

"Well, it was worth a try." Julian smiled, wishing he could ease her pain in some way, but knowing he couldn't.

And that, for some unexplained reason, haunted him more than he cared to consider.

"Thank you for staying," Sophia mouthed.

"No problem," Charlie said. "I didn't have plans. Happy to ask the nurse your questions."

"I'm sorry they're having to get the charge nurse and you have to wait." Sophia had just about enough of questions with no answers. She was tired of being helpless.

"As I said before, I have no plans, so it's not a big deal." Charlie leaned back in the chair, flipping her full auburn hair over her shoulder.

Sophia realized she knew nothing about the person who had so graciously been acting as her voice. "What do you do? I mean, besides read lips?"

"Actually, reading lips is my job." Charlie laughed. It was a husky, throaty laugh.

Sophia decided it suited her.

"I'm a professional lip reader. I mainly work for a variety of law enforcement agencies in the area—FBI, the state police, local sheriff offices—to help cases with surveillance videos and other types of interviews. On occasion, I've ventured in to help in other cases."

"Like mine?"

Charlie nodded. "Like yours."

It could be interesting. "Are you deaf?" Sophia mouthed.

Charlie laughed again. Sophia could get used to the sound. "No, I'm not deaf. My older brother was, so I grew up learning to sign before I spoke and learning to read lips before I could read books." She shrugged. "I enjoy helping others and I'm good at it, so I became a professional lip reader/translator."

"Well, I appreciate you." It was nice to *talk* to someone. Especially a female.

In Sophia's life, she didn't make girlfriends because she was always too busy practicing in the gym or heading to a competition. She couldn't count other gymnasts as friends, either, because at the end of the day, they were competition. Gymnastics could be a ruthless industry, full of backstabbers and selfish climbers who used people to get to the next level. Not exactly girls you wanted to share your innermost thoughts with. Sophia had learned early in the game not to try and become best friends with the other girls. It only led to painful disappointments.

"You're so welcome, Sophia." Charlie leaned forward in the chair. "I heard Alena came back to see you." It was a statement, but the lilt at the last word made it sound like a question.

Sophia nodded. "Unfortunately, she did. I'm sure Julian or Brody told you. I was what caused my mother and Alena's estrangement. Alena wanted my mother to abort me and keep her dancing career, and my mother refused."

"Well, thank the good Lord she did."

Relief filled Sophia. Sometimes, it was hard to tell if someone was a Christian, but knowing this woman she'd felt such a connection to was a believer made Sophia extremely happy. She went on to replay the conversation to Charlie, filling her in even on the most painful admissions.

"Wow. I'm so sorry, Sophia. It's rough. On top of everything else you're having to deal with right now."

"I understand why *Mamochka* lied and told me Alena was dead. She knew if she admitted Alena demanded I be aborted, it would hurt me, but she knew if I knew Alena was alive, I'd ask endless questions about her until the truth came out. I know she was trying to protect me, trying to spare my feelings, but I just feel so . . . betrayed by my mother."

"I understand. I would think as a mother, she'd do anything to protect her child." Charlie smiled. "Protect you."

"But she also taught me lying was wrong. Even the little white lies to save someone's feelings from being hurt. I feel like now I have to question every life lesson she told me. Was she teaching me to do as she said, not as she did? Didn't she hold herself to the same standards as she taught me? Did she teach me one way, but act in a totally different manner?" Sophia shook her head as the confusion spun a cobweb around her mind.

"I can only imagine how confusing this must all be. I'd drive myself crazy with all the possibilities."

"I know." Sophia had grown weary of trying to figure things out. After she had refused to open her eyes and look at Alena, the woman had finally gotten the hint and left. She'd made sure she shook her head strongly when the police officer guarding the door asked if he should let Alena back in.

"You know, I can see how Alena felt the way she did. She'd given up everything—her home, her husband, her entire life—for her daughter's dancing, only to feel like her daughter threw it all away." Sophia let out a heavy sigh. "She wasn't right, of course, but in a warped way, I can kinda understand how she felt betrayed, too."

"So she feels betrayed by what she believes is her daughter's selfishness. Your mother feels betrayed by her mother who refused to accept her love and her child. And you feel betrayed by both of them."

Sophia nodded. "Exactly. But even more, I'm seeing a pattern. Alena sacrificed everything for my mother's success in dancing.

Hired the best instructors. Worked at odd jobs so she could afford the dance studios, but also have a flexible schedule so she could take her to the classes. They had their estrangement and never spoke again. But my mother did much of the same thing for me. She sacrificed a lot to pay for my gymnastics. She hired the best coaches. Worked when she didn't feel like it at the studio to pay for me to go to the best gym here, then paid for me to get to go to the gym I now train from."

"But you love gymnastics, yes?" Charlie asked.

"Yes, but my mother loved dancing. Everything about her screamed of her love for ballet. Her mother gave up everything for her to dance. My mother gave up everything—even her true love of being a ballerina—for me."

"Because she loved your father and you. She wanted a family. It was her choice."

"Maybe." But Sophia couldn't help but wonder if her mother had regretted her choice. Especially after Sophia's father died.

"Good evening." The charge nurse came into the room, carrying Sophia's chart. "I understand you have some questions about your treatment?"

Charlie stood. "I'm Charlie Wallace, Sophia's lip reader. She has some questions. I'll translate exactly what she's asking, okay?"

The nurse nodded.

Charlie stared at Sophia.

"Dr. Rhoads had told me yesterday that when the swelling went down in my throat, I could eat. Does my chart have any indication when it could happen?"

The nurse flipped pages. "Looks like the swelling hadn't gone down enough when he examined you this morning." She looked up from the chart. "Are you hungry?"

Sophia nodded. All afternoon, her stomach had made the loudest rumblings.

"I'll make a note for the doctor to review it in the morning. How is your pain with your throat tonight?"

Sophia swallowed. It didn't feel like she was trying to eat razor blades. "Better."

The nurse scribbled.

"I haven't seen the hand surgeon. Shouldn't I have?"

Again, the nurse flipped through papers in the chart. "Your surgery was early Friday morning. Your surgeon has reviewed your chart notes several times."

"But he hasn't been here to see me. To answer my questions."

"He should be in Monday morning. If you'd like, I can make a note you request to see him during rounds."

Sophia rolled her eyes at Charlie.

"Please do."

The nurse scribbled, then looked up. "Anything else?"

She wasn't rude, exactly, but Sophia got the distinct feeling the nurse felt like she had more important things to do than answer her questions. "Is there any indication when I can get up and walk?"

"According to your chart, your pelvis should only need one more day of rest. I would expect Dr. Rhoads will talk to you about that tomorrow."

"What time does the doctor usually make rounds on Sunday?" Charlie asked, although Sophia hadn't.

"Oh, Dr. Rhoads is normally on the floor around ten or so on Sundays."

"Good. Thank you for your time."

The nurse nodded and left.

Sophia looked at Charlie. "That was interesting," she mouthed.

"Rude, much?" Charlie laughed. "I'll be here tomorrow morning when your doctor makes rounds so I can talk for you."

"Oh, I don't want to be a bother." But inside, Sophia was pleased Charlie would be able to translate for her.

"Nonsense. I'm happy to help." Charlie stood and squeezed Sophia's foot. "I'll see you in the morning. Try to get some rest, okay?"

Once Charlie left, Sophia closed her eyes. *God, I'm really struggling. With everything. You know my heart. You know my pain. Lord, please give me comfort. Please.*

7

"Why am I not surprised you're here so bright and early?"

Julian looked up from his monitor and smiled at his partner. "Early bird gets the worm, you know."

Brody dropped into his chair across the desks from him. "Anything new to report?"

"Nothing yet. I've called forensics and they're going as fast as they can, but there's nothing concrete yet." He leaned back in his chair and reached for his keychain. "How about you?"

"I've sent a unit over to the crime scene to see if they can find a diary or journal of Nina's."

"Doubtful, but we can always hope."

"Oh, and I got the background check on Alena Borin." Brody waved a folder.

Julian dropped his keychain and reached for his notebook and pen. "Give me the edited version."

"Alena Borin, sixty-one, moved to the United States from Russia twenty-eight years ago on a special work visa, leaving behind her husband, Vlad Borin. They never divorced, despite her leaving him. And I do mean leaving him. When she left the motherland, she never returned. She applied for American citizenship for herself and her daughter, Nina Borin, three years after moving to the United States. They lived in D.C. for five years before moving to New York City. They only lived there before she moved to Arkansas. Currently lives in Hot Springs. No full-time job, but the quilts she makes are very sought after."

"That's it?"

Brody nodded. "Pretty much. What's interesting is she was a dancer in her youth, too. Not as accomplished as her daughter. From what I understand, she had the drive and determination, just not the talent. At least, it's what I gathered from the statements pulled in the check."

"Interesting." Julian set down his pen and grabbed his keychain. "Sounds like maybe she pushed Nina, trying to live her own dreams through her daughter."

"Could be. Sad. I see those kinds of parents all the time."

"It's a shame." He couldn't stop thinking about what Sophia had shared with them about Alena. "Still, it's hard to believe someone would want their grandchild aborted just so their child could continue on as a ballerina. Harsh."

"It's hard for us Americans to think that way. We're geared toward family and children. Other countries don't have the same ideals. I'm not saying either way is right or wrong, it's just the way it is. In Russia, to be a prima ballerina is huge. It's like a ticket to more opportunities. A chance to experience the world. I would imagine Alena wanted Nina to have all the best opportunities that came along."

Julian stopped spinning the keychain. "You sound like you speak from experience."

"Not exactly. My sister had a good friend in the Russian troupe. Those people are truly dedicated. She thought my sister was crazy for quitting dance to go to college. It's a different environment."

"I guess." Julian just couldn't wrap his mind around the idea. He opened the case file and stared at the newspaper article on Sophia.

"Did you get Nina's background check back?" Brody asked.

Julian shook his head, his attention still focused on Sophia's picture. "Wasn't in our box or on our desks when I came in." He was still so taken with the blissful expression she wore.

Brody lifted the phone and requested the full background file on Nina be sent to them as soon as possible.

Even Sophia's posture exuded pleasure. She stood on the hearth, her awards glistening on the mantle against the backdrop of an odd quilted tapestry. The—

Julian flipped through the file to the crime scene photos. He pulled out the living room shot and laid it beside the newspaper article.

"What?" Brody asked.

"There's this odd looking quilted tapestry in this photo, taken at the crime scene just last week. I don't see it amid the shambles in the crime scene photos."

Brody came around the desks and looked over Julian's shoulder. "I don't see it either."

"It could be a lead."

"Or, it could be that it's there and we just don't see it. It might be mingled in with the shards from the other tapestries or curtains."

Julian shrugged.

"Or it could be in one of the evidence boxes or somewhere else in the house."

"Maybe." But Julian *felt* in his gut this was a lead. "We should have someone look through the evidence boxes and ask Sophia about it."

"Of course. I'll get someone to look in evidence." Brody lifted his phone and dialed.

Julian's phone rang. He snatched it up. "Homicide, Detective Frazier."

"This is Lee in forensics. Wanted to let you know your hunch paid off."

Finally! "Really?"

"Yes, sir. We found droplets of foreign matter on Nina Montgomery's shirt, consistent with sweat droplets. We're starting the DNA testing now."

"Great. How long before you have something?"

"It varies, sir, but I've put a rush on it so we should have it ready to load into CODIS within forty-eight hours."

"Thanks, Lee. I appreciate it." Julian hung up the phone and told his partner the good news.

"Finally, a solid lead."

"Today just might be our lucky day." Julian updated the case file notes.

"Well, it *is* Sunday."

Julian stabbed his pen into his pencil holder on his desk. "You don't buy into all the religious mumbo-jumbo, do you?"

Brody arched a single eyebrow. "Ah, so you aren't a believer?"

Julian shook his head. "To each his own, but I stopped buying into the whole 'great and powerful God of everything' about the same time I stopped believing justice always prevailed."

"Yeah, most cops are jaded. We see too much of the ugly stuff." Brody sat on the edge of Julian's desk.

Julian hadn't missed the *most cops* distinction. "But not you? You're a Christian?"

Brody chuckled and moved to sit behind his own desk. "I am. It's okay, though. It's not a bad thing like the way you say it."

"I'm sorry. No offense."

"None taken." Brody shrugged. "We all have to make our own choices. I just choose to believe in God."

At one time, Julian could have agreed with him. But ever since Eli had died . . . there was no sense. No logic. And if there was a God, if He allowed all this senseless violence to keep happening, well, He wasn't such a great God.

"I'm getting some coffee. You want a cup?" Brody asked, standing.

"That nasty stuff?" Julian wrinkled his nose, made a face, then laughed. "Nah, man. Thanks, but I don't think so. That stuff is deadly."

"It puts hair on your chest." Brody laughed as he left.

Julian stared after him. He'd learned more about Brody in the last couple of days than he'd known about him in the last six weeks since becoming partners. It was a little nice to fall back into a routine of having a trusted person to confide in, but Julian knew he couldn't let himself get in too deep. Friendships, while great, could pull the rug out from under you when they were ripped away without warning.

His cell rang. He checked the caller ID. "Hey, Charlie. How's everything with you?"

"Good. I'm on my way to the hospital to see Sophia."

Julian froze. "Is something wrong?"

"No, I just told her I'd come this morning to be there when her doctor makes rounds, so I could ask some specific questions for her."

"Good." He glanced at the pictures in the open case file. "Can you stay for a while? I have a couple of questions for Sophia. If you don't mind."

"Hey, I'm on your payroll, Frazier." Her chuckle made him smile.

"Yeah, you are, so why are you calling me?"

"Just wanted to touch base with you. See if you have any updates."

"Nothing concrete yet." He couldn't tell her about the sweat. While on retainer for the police department, she wasn't actually on the force. At this point, he couldn't even tell Sophia. Not until they had something.

"Okay. Guess I'll see you in a bit. Bye."

Julian put his cell back in its holder on his belt, thinking about Charlie. He'd met her through her brother, who had been a good friend of Eli's. Scott was a great mechanic, who helped Eli restore old cars. Eli had introduced Julian to Scott when they'd started work on the Charger's restoration. Julian had liked the deaf man immediately. He'd liked his sister even more the first time he met Charlie.

Although no one at the force—not now anyway, since Eli was gone—knew Julian had actually gone out with Charlie a couple of times. No denying she was a beautiful woman, but there just hadn't been any chemistry between them. They'd decided they were better off as friends than as a couple and had been good buddies for a couple of years now. Despite their having dated, Charlie was always looking to fix Julian up on some blind date or another. She said he was too hardened and needed a woman to soften him up.

Brody joined him. "I'm going to go interview Nina's neighbors again. See if anyone knows anything about a scooter or golf cart or whatever Sophia might have heard before the attack."

Julian nodded. "Good idea. Maybe it will give us a suspect."

Brody left without another word, leaving Julian alone with his disturbing relationship thoughts. He preferred to keep his feelings under wraps, thank you very much. Besides, he didn't have time for dating. He was married to his work. To saving lives and keeping the streets safe for the good people in his town.

Hey, it sounded good, right?

Sophia closed her mouth and stared as Dr. Rhoads stuck his penlight back in his jacket pocket.

"Well?" she mouthed and Charlie spoke.

"Looks like the swelling has continued to go down. The charge nurse left a note you were hungry?"

"Yes."

He looked over her chart again. "If you feel ready, we can remove the feeding tube. Your throat will be very sore, and I'd advise you not to try and talk for at least another day or so. You'll be on a strictly liquid diet at least for twenty-four hours, but if you have no problems and I see no sign of infection, you should be able to start eating and talking, even if it's a whisper, by Tuesday. We can further evaluate then. How's that sound?"

"Wonderful, Dr. Rhoads. Thank you."

"We'll keep the humidifier running, though. Just as a precaution against crust formation and transient ciliary dysfunction." He smiled at Sophia. "Now, I also see you had some questions about getting up and about?"

Sophia nodded.

"Are you having any pain in your pelvic region?"

She shook her head.

He set her chart on the table and gently probed her hips and abdomen. "Does this hurt?"

Again she shook her head.

"Here?"

"No."

"Now?"

"Nothing."

He straightened and reached for her chart. "Excellent. After the feeding tube's removed, I'll order the catheter removed. Then you can let the nurses help you up. While you should take it easy today, you can at least move around the room a little. You'll have to be careful not to lose your balance, and you can't walk around if someone isn't in here with you, do you understand? With your pain medication, you're a little groggy. We can't take a chance on you falling."

"Yes. I won't."

The doctor wrote on the chart. "The stitches used on your face and head are dissolvable, so they won't require attention for removal. You may begin to notice a tightening sensation and itching in those areas over the next day or so before they start to dissolve. That's completely normal."

She nodded. She'd wondered if she'd imagined the itching she'd felt during the night.

"The bruising and swelling on your face are also resolving as they should. I see no signs of any infection."

Well, this was good news.

"What about my hands?"

"Your surgeon has been receiving the nurses' notes every time they change your bandages and clean your wounds. He should be by to see you sometime tomorrow morning."

"What do you think?"

Dr. Rhoads smiled and closed her chart, handing it to the nurse who shadowed him. "I think you're a lucky young lady to be alive. Your surgeon will be by tomorrow to discuss your hands. Now, I'll review your progress after the feeding tube is removed and you've gotten up. You might have wished you took another day to rest up."

"No, I won't."

"Okay then." He pointed at the nurse. "They'll be back in a few minutes to take out the feeding tube."

"Thank you, Dr. Rhoads." Sophia smiled at Charlie as the doctor left the room.

"Excited to get the tube out?" Charlie asked as the hospital room door closed.

"You have no idea."

Charlie smiled. "Actually, I do. I was in a car accident a couple of years ago and had a feeding tube." She shuddered. "Was worse than the cast."

"I understand." Sophia mouthed.

The door whooshed open and the nurse who had been trailing Dr. Rhoads came in. "Okay, we're going to take the feeding tube out now, then your catheter. Going tubeless." She laughed at her own joke.

Charlie stood. "I think that's my cue to leave."

"Thank you for coming." Sophia smiled.

"Oh. I talked with Julian earlier. He's coming by to ask you some new questions, so I'll stay and translate. I'll just run down to the cafeteria and grab a snack." Charlie patted her foot. "I'll be back in to see the tubeless you soon."

So, Julian was coming by again? Sophia struggled to pay attention to what the nurse was telling her, but it was hard to do when all she could think about was the case.

More questions? Did it mean they had a lead?

"Okay, hon, let's get you sitting as upright as possible," the nurse said as she pressed buttons and the bed hummed in movement.

Sophia's heartbeat quickened. She couldn't wait to get this tube out of her nose.

"I'm going to remove the tape holding the tube in place. It'll feel like pulling off a big Band-Aid." The nurse pressed her cold fingers against Sophia's face and pried the tape off.

Sophia cringed.

"Sorry. There's always a little sting."

A little sting? Was she kidding? It was like pulling off a layer of skin on her already sore face.

"Now, this next part is going to be a bit uncomfortable. You'll feel pressure as I gently pull the tube out." The nurse took hold of the tube just below where the tape had been. "I know the instinct is to get it out fast and furious, but we have to take a little extra care and go a little slower to make sure the tube doesn't stretch and break."

Stretch and break?

The nurse continued. "Now, once the end of the tube gets near the top of the esophagus, I'll pause for a minute to give you a moment to rest. Okay?"

Not really, but Sophia didn't see any other options. She gave a nod and closed her eyes, pinching them tight.

"Just try to breathe normally through your mouth." The nurse pulled the tube. Uncomfortable? No. It was more like a razor blade snaking up her throat. Sophia concentrated on breathing with her mouth open.

How long was this process supposed to take? Sophia decided to keep her mind occupied. Concentrate on something else. She could count. One . . .

Another inch of tube crept out. Heat rushed to Sophia's face.

Two . . .

How long was the tube anyway?

Three . . .

Was it to the top of the esophagus yet? She curled her toes as she kept her eyes clamped tight, denying the tears threatening to escape.

Four . . .

Sweet Lord, please give me strength.

Five . . .

The nurse stopped tugging. "Okay. We're at the top of the esophagus. Take a minute to rest your throat. Keep breathing through your mouth as you can. You're doing great."

Doing great, huh? Sophia swallowed. Surprisingly, it didn't hurt nearly as bad as she'd thought. She'd expected the pain to be excruciating. Maybe, just maybe, she could handle this after all.

The nurse smiled at her. "Are you ready?"

How was she supposed to answer? How could she be ready for something she didn't know what to expect?

"We'll move much faster this time as I pull the tube through your oropharynx and out through your nose," the nurse continued.

"This may stimulate your gag reflex, but only temporarily until the tube is out." She patted Sophia's shoulder. "Ready?"

No time like the present. Sophia nodded.

The nurse pulled and Sophia could have sworn she saw stars just before she wanted to throw up.

"You did great." The nurse wound the tube and stuck it in a bag. "You just rest a bit. I'm going to get things straightened up, then we'll get the catheter out. I'll rewrap your hands so you'll be able to slip on gloves to protect the gauze to use the restroom."

Oh, joy.

8

Sophia turned her head to look as Julian walked into her hospital room. "Hi, Sophia." He nodded at Charlie.

"Hi, Detective Frazier," Sophia mouthed and Charlie said.

"You're looking much better this afternoon." And she did. The tube was gone from her nose and she looked more aware. More focused.

"Thanks. I'm doing better. The doctor's even going to let me get up and walk around the room later this afternoon."

"Awesome." Julian set his folder on her bedside table and pulled a chair closer to the side of her bed. "Hey, Charlie. Thanks for staying."

"No problem," Charlie smiled at him. "Sophia and I were able to listen to the podcast of my church's services from this morning."

It seemed all of a sudden, he was surrounded by Christians. He looked back at Sophia. "Well . . . good."

"Do you have a lead?" Charlie asked for Sophia.

He shook his head. "Just double-checking every detail we can and following every lead." He grabbed his folder and opened it. "I wanted to ask you something." He held up an article in the Arkansas state paper with the interview and photo of her a week ago. "Do you remember this?"

She nodded.

He pointed to the tapestry hanging over the mantle. "Can you tell me what this is?"

"It's *Mamochka's* quilt. Made from her dance costumes." Her eyes grew wider, looking enormous against her still swollen and bruised face. It led to her appearance of fragility. "Did you find it?"

The black-and-white newspaper photograph didn't give enough detail. Too grainy. "We've looked and can't find it. We're checking the evidence boxes now."

"That's because *Mamochka* put it up for safekeeping after the picture was printed."

A quilt put away for safety's sake after a photograph being in the paper? "I'm not sure I understand, Sophia."

"I conducted the interview while my mother was out. She knew I was giving the interview, but didn't realize they'd take photographs of me until she saw the paper." Sophia blinked, staring at the paper for a long moment before returning her focus to him. "I remember when she saw the paper. She was furious. So angry."

"Why?" He couldn't understand what would make Nina so angry.

"I don't know. She wouldn't tell me. She took the quilt off its hanger and hid it in her closet."

"She hid it in her closet?"

Sophia nodded. "My mother . . . well, *Mamochka* could be a little odd at times. She often hid things of sentimental value."

"I'm guessing a quilt would only be worth sentimental value."

"You'd be wrong." Charlie shook her head. "Sorry, that's me talking, not Sophia."

"What do you mean?"

"I have a friend who collects quilts, and some of the old ones can be worth quite a bit of money. One sold several years ago for over two hundred and fifty thousand dollars at auction."

"Two hundred and—" Julian shook his head. "You're messing with me."

"No, I'm serious. It was a quilt from the Civil War era, but some other quilts are worth quite a bit of money."

He had no idea.

"Did you know there's even an International Quilt Study Center housed at the University of Nebraska?" Charlie asked. "There are even such professions as quilt appraisers."

Learned something new every day. He looked at Sophia. "Was your mother's quilt old?"

"Not terribly. I don't think *Mamochka's* quilt was valuable to others. It was made from her ballet costumes." Sophia smiled sadly, as Charlie spoke for her. "She even let me quilt some of the pieces with her when I was younger. As we worked, she'd tell me about her performance wearing each of the costumes."

Julian's cell phone vibrated. He glanced at the caller ID: Brody. "Excuse me a moment, please. I need to take this." He stepped out into the hall. "Whatcha got?"

"Talked with the neighbors again. Nobody heard anything like a scooter or golf cart just prior to the attack. But one of the neighbors is still out of town until tomorrow."

"So, another dead end?"

"We'll keep checking. Also, just heard from the uni in evidence. No sign of the tapestry."

"I'm at the hospital with Sophia now. It's a quilt."

"I'll double-check with evidence on it. Do you think it's what they were after?"

Sophia didn't think her mother's quilt was worth hundreds of thousands of dollars, which was probably true, but who knew how valuable a quilt made by one of Russia's former prima ballerinas with costume materials could be. Could be worth enough for motive. "Maybe. Sophia says Nina took it off the wall and hid it in her bedroom closet after the newspaper picture."

"I'm still in the neighborhood so I can head over to the house and look for it. Can you ask Sophia if she has any idea of where in Nina's bedroom it might be?"

"Sure. Hang on." Julian stepped back into Sophia's room where she and Charlie were smiling. "Sophia, do you know where your mother hid things in her closet?"

Sophia nodded and Charlie spoke what she mouthed. "On the right hand side of the closet, near the end, but not at the end, there are two hangers, each with large, bulky sweaters. *Mamochka* hung things on the hangers under those sweaters."

"Thanks." Julian relayed the information to Brody.

"Got it. On my way now. If I find it, I'll bring it in for testing."

Julian glanced at Sophia's eyes. They held such an expression of hope and grief, both at the same time. It was unnerving what she did to him so effortlessly. "If you do, put a rush on forensics." The least he could do was get something so sentimental to Sophia back as quickly as possible. It might help ease her grief.

"You got it." Brody, in his usual fashion, hung up.

Replacing his cell to the holder on his hip, Julian moved back to Sophia's bedside. "What else can you tell me about the quilt?"

"Well, it's a Hidden Star pattern around the border, with the centerpiece being almost the full bodice of one costume: the Sugar Plum Fairy from the *Nutcracker*. Each of the squares on the border are all pieces from her costumes."

"Costumes from what dances, if you know?"

"Let's see, she danced as the title role in *Cinderella*—the Rostislav Zakharov choreographed version, she was Kitri in *Don Quixote*, she was the Lilac Fairy in *La Belle au Bois Dormant*, also known as *The Sleeping Beauty* ballet, and she was Nikiya in Petipa's *La Bayadère*, commonly called *The Temple Dancer*."

Julian wrote as Charlie spoke for Sophia, whose eyes were closed, yet her face wore the most peaceful expression. He tightened his hold on his pencil, keeping his hands on task to stop them from reaching out and smoothing the lock of hair curling around her cheekbone. Despite the careful stitching on the cut atop the cheekbone, there'd most likely still be a scar. It'd be slight, and kinda sexy, actually, if he didn't know what caused the blemish on her perfect skin.

No! He needed to concentrate. All this talk of ballet seemed to be doing a number on his fanciful imagination. "What else?"

"She also danced the title role in *Giselle.* It was one of her best performances, at least that's what she always said." Sophia opened her eyes. "She danced as Juliet in *Romeo and Juliet*, danced the role of Swanilda in *Coppélia*, and was the Black Swan in *Swan Lake.*"

Julian wasn't a ballet watcher, not by any standards, but even he recognized the names of the some of the most famous ballets in the world, and that Nina Borin had the lead and title roles in many of them, well, it spoke volumes about how truly talented of a dancer she'd been.

He could almost—almost, but not quite, understand why Alena hadn't wanted her daughter to throw away her career, even for a child.

With those famous roles, maybe the quilt was worth more than Sophia assumed.

"There are many more, but without seeing the quilt, I can't remember."

He patted her shoulder. "No, this is great. Just what I needed." Had he just said that out loud? "We. What we needed." He should never touch her again. Made his mind jumble.

Charlie's stare locked onto him. Heat marched up the back of his neck.

A nurse pushed open the door. "Are you about ready to get up and walk around for a bit?"

Sophia smiled and nodded.

"Oh, yes," Charlie said for her.

Julian grabbed his folder. "I'll get out of here and give you some privacy."

"Will you let me know if you find the quilt?"

"I will. If Brody finds it, I'll let you know."

Charlie shot him a knowing look as he turned to go. He'd have to answer for his slip later. Much later, if he could manage it.

<hr />

After her years and years of physical exertion and strength endurance training, who knew making one little lap around a small hospital room could wear her completely out?

Now back in her bed, Sophia relaxed in the solitude. Her stomach growled and she smiled to herself. She'd worked up an appetite. The nurse had promised to bring her some chicken broth and gelatin for dinner. Sophia was excited about getting to have food, even if it was only liquids, to actually taste something again. However, she hated to be at the mercy of others to feed her. At least, getting up and being able to walk a little made her feel like she'd regained a bit of her independence back.

Along the same vein, she knew she needed to find a way to get in touch with Coach Douglas. Soon. He needed to contact her alternate and get her to the gym in Huntsville, so she could start training with the rest of the team.

Grief as real as what she felt over losing *Mamochka* filled her with such despair. She'd trained and sacrificed all her life to make the Olympic team, to go for the gold. She'd worked hard and foregone a regular life, and she'd achieved the main step toward her goal—making the team. It'd been almost eighteen years of preparation, dedication, blood, sweat, and tears to get this far. And now? Well . . . now she had nothing.

No career. No mother. Nothing.

She'd even skipped college to focus on her gymnastics training. Sophia had nothing to fall back on. No home. No family. In preparation for the Olympic training, she'd even released her apartment back in Plano, so she didn't even have a place to live. There was no way she'd go back to her mother's. Not after what happened.

Nothing.

The door eased open and Detective Julian Frazier stuck his head into the room. "May I come in?"

She nodded. It was wrong how Sophia's heart hiccupped over his presence, but she blushed anyway. Good thing her face was still swollen so he couldn't detect the blushing.

At least she hoped not.

He stood beside her bed. "It's a little harder without Charlie here, isn't it?"

She nodded. The constant humming of the humidifier filled the awkward silence. Maybe she could try to talk. No, Dr. Rhoads had told her not to even try until Tuesday or she could permanently damage her vocal chords. Just being unable to speak these past three days had convinced Sophia she'd do whatever the doctor told her to protect her ability to speak.

"I just wanted you to know Brody found the quilt in your mother's closet. Forensics is going over it now, but as soon as they're done, I'll release it back to you." He smiled and warmth fanned out from her chest. "I know it's important to you for sentimental value."

"Thank you," she mouthed.

"You're welcome."

Her nurse came in, carrying a syringe. "Don't mind me. I'm just going to slip your medication in your IV and check your stats. I'll be in and out in a jiffy." She did just that, smiled at Sophia, then rushed out.

An awkward silence hung in the air.

Julian straightened. "My officer outside tells me they'll be moving you out of the critical care unit."

She nodded. Dr. Rhoads had come by when she was up walking and had decided she could be moved to a regular room tomorrow. And he'd told her the hand surgeon should be by to see her tomorrow morning as well. Big day for her.

"I don't want you to worry. We'll be keeping a uniformed officer posted outside your door whatever floor you're on, okay?"

She smiled. His concern for her safety and well-being was probably just part of his job since she was his only witness to his case, but it made her feel protected. Safe.

One of the hospital workers came into the room, carrying a tray. "Here's your broth and gelatin, as ordered." She set the tray on the adjustable table. "We're a little shorthanded right now, so I'm glad you have someone here to feed you. Otherwise, you'd have to wait a good bit." And before Sophia could think of a way to protest, the worker was gone.

"Um." Julian looked as uncomfortable as Sophia felt.

She shook her head.

"You aren't hungry?"

She shrugged, unable to lie. How could she tell him it would be mortifying for him to feed her?

Her stomach picked just then to growl again. Loudly.

Julian chuckled. "Guess that's one way to answer." He lifted the lid off the pink tray to reveal a large covered cup and a small bowl of red gelatin. "Oh, yummy." He pulled off the cover of the large cup and steam wafted into the air.

The smell wrapped around Sophia's senses and her stomach rumbled again in reply.

Julian laughed again. "Okay, okay. I'm hurrying." He glanced around the room, then grabbed the clean hand towel by the sink. He gently laid it over her chest, shoulder-to-shoulder. "I'm not

experienced in feeding someone else, so I want to make sure anything I spill on you won't burn you."

Yep, she was beyond horrified at the moment, but what
could she do? She was hungry—starving—and her stomach had
announced the fact. Twice. She couldn't very well lie and say she
didn't want anything. Her mouth watered at the aroma filling her
nostrils. She'd never imagined chicken broth could be so appetiz-
ing. Right now, it smelled just as good as a fat, juicy T-bone grilled
to perfection.

Her stomach grumbled again.

Julian grabbed the plastic spoon and lifted the large cup. "Okay,
I'm going to do my best to get more of this in you than on you, but
understand I'm probably not too good at this."

She smiled, nodding.

He leaned closer, close enough she could detect the subtle
undertones of men's aftershave. Spicy and alluring.

Sophia gave herself a strong, mental shake. Could her humilia-
tion get any worse? She needed to keep her mind off the detective's
appeal and on the reason for his being here—he was working her
mother's murder.

The thought sobered her right up.

Julian dipped the spoon into the broth, then lifted it out. Steam
shimmered above the spoon. Ever so gently, he blew on the broth in
the spoon, before moving it slowly to her mouth.

Her heart pounding for inexplicable reasons, Sophia parted her
lips and let him ease the broth between her swollen lips, his eyes
never leaving her mouth.

At first, the hot broth burnt going down her throat, and she
could feel it going all the way down into her stomach. But it was
good. Her tastebuds sat up at attention. Her stomach demanded
more, rumbling loudly.

Julian dropped his gaze to the bowl. "Guess you answered my unasked question of whether it's any good." Under the golden hue of his skin, a reddish blush filled his face.

Was he embarrassed, or . . . ? Could he be feeling the same unexplained attraction she didn't want to admit she felt?

"Here." He lifted the spoon to her mouth again. This time, the broth didn't burn at all. To be a liquid, it felt filling. Felt good. It was almost as if she could feel herself getting stronger.

"I guess I could talk to you about the case while you eat, huh?" Julian kept feeding her, blowing the broth with each spoonful so it wouldn't be too hot.

His attention warmed her as quickly and thoroughly as the broth.

"As I said, Brody found the quilt. He also found some other things under those sweaters. An Air Force uniform for one."

Sophia's heart clenched. She'd seen her father's uniform only a handful of times in her life, but each time, *Mamochka* had been in the privacy of her bedroom, clutching it to her chest and crying. Sophia had never made her presence known, even at a young age, realizing she'd be intruding on a private and personal moment.

"I'm assuming it belonged to your father?" Julian's voice was soft and low.

She nodded, as she accepted another spoonful of chicken broth.

"Brody didn't disturb it." He blew on the spoon. "He also found a ballet costume."

That was new. Sophia swallowed and shrugged.

"You didn't know about it?" he asked as he fed her another bite. She shook her head.

"I'll ask forensics to put a rush on it as well, so I can bring it by for you to look at it."

She nodded and took another spoonful. Her stomach clenched as the liquid gurgled. Getting something on an empty stomach made all sorts of interesting noises. Sophia's face burned as the sounds echoed across the room over the humming of the humidifier.

The plastic spoon grated against the cup. "Okay, this is the last bite." Julian didn't blow on it before feeding it to her. It'd cooled enough.

She licked her lips and took the last spoonful.

He set down the cup and lifted the little bowl of red Jell-O. "Ready for this?"

She nodded. Even though she'd finished off the entire big cup of chicken broth, she felt like she could eat a whole cow.

Gently, he put a half a spoonful of the gelatin in her mouth. The sweet coolness was such a contrast to the hot and salty broth, she shivered.

Julian's expression softened even more, enough that it made her pulse spike. "I'm sorry," he said as he set down the bowl and spoon and eased the towel from her chest. "I didn't realize you'd gotten chilled, but I should have. What with the hot, then the cold." He grabbed the little blanket folded at the foot of her bed and snuggled it over her, covering her shoulders. "Is that better?"

Warmth oozed through her, and she suddenly felt sleepy. She yawned.

Julian laughed. "Am I boring you?"

Embarrassment pushed a heated blush across her cheeks. She shook her head even as she fought against another yawn. The medication must have kicked in, making her sleepy, on top of finally getting something warm on her stomach.

"How about we save the rest of the Jell-O for later?" Julian asked.

She nodded. Then yawned again.

He ducked his head, almost hiding his grin, but Sophia caught a peek of it, as he covered the bowl and set the tray aside. He had a nice smile, especially when it reached his eyes. "There. All done." He stood awkwardly beside her bed, like a kid who didn't quite know how to act around her. "Well, I'll let you get some rest. I'll see you tomorrow."

"Thank you," she mouthed.

"You're welcome."

"Good night."

He smiled and his whole face lit up. "Goodnight to you, too." His grin spread. "Hey, maybe I'll replace Charlie as a lip reader, huh?"

She grinned, then yawned.

Julian chuckled and gave her shoulder a little squeeze. "Sweet dreams."

She wanted to talk to him, but her eyes were just . . .

so . . .

heavy.

9

W e have the report on Nina Borin Montgomery and Sophia."
That was Brody's greeting as Julian walked into the station early
Monday morning.

"Well, tell me what you're dying to tell me." Julian plopped into
his chair and leaned back, lacing his fingers together behind his
head. "I'm ready."

Brody grinned and shook his head. "Nina Montgomery, born
Borin, aged forty at the time of death. Studied dance from the time
she was four at the Vaganova Ballet Academy in St. Petersburg,
Russia. At the age of eleven, her high-profile talent was cemented
by being selected to dance the role of Little Radish in *Cipollino*.
This was the official launch of her career, as the performance made
her talent the talk of Moscow and garnered her a feature in the
most respected industry publication, *Dance Magazine*."

Julian paid close attention, wondering if Sophia was aware of all
her mother's roles.

Brody continued. "Wanting more opportunities for her
daughter, Alena moved with Nina from Russia to the States—
Washington, D.C.—twenty-eight years ago for Nina to attend the
Kirov Academy of Ballet. She was only twelve, but Nina quickly

became a prima ballerina when she performed as the Sea Princess in *The Little Humpbacked Horse*."

The sounds of the police station coming to life as the start of shift drew nearer caused Julian to sit up straighter, so he could hear his partner better.

"She graduated at seventeen and was offered a spot with the New York City Ballet Company. She accepted and moved with her mother to New York. Her career seemed to take off. There are numerous articles and features in all the popular dance media outlets of her performances in various ballets. Great reviews. She was romantically linked, briefly, with Dimitri Taras, a dancer with the same company. Wealthy, but with a violent reputation."

Interesting. Julian couldn't help but wonder if Dimitri had ever popped back up in Nina's life.

"Then suddenly, Nina got married to one Lance Montgomery, airman first class, United States Air Force. Dropped out of the dance world entirely. Moved to Little Rock, Arkansas, since Lance was stationed at the Little Rock base and, soon after, had a baby girl. Sophia."

Julian spun his key chain around his finger as he listened.

"When Sophia was two, Lance was killed in a plane crash. Nina received approximately two hundred thousand dollars in life insurance benefits. She bought a small home here in Hot Springs Village as well as a building she turned into a dance studio. After funeral costs and the purchases, she had little life insurance money left. Her dance studio did well, supporting Nina and little Sophia."

It was hard for Julian to comprehend the hardship Sophia's mother had gone through at such a young age.

"When Sophia was still little, Nina enrolled her in gymnastics. At first, just our local gym where Nina bartered dance lessons for the gym owner's daughter in exchange for Sophia's lessons. Soon, it became evident to many that little Sophia had a natural talent for the sport. Nina got her better gym access and began hiring personal trainers."

"Was the dance studio doing that well?" Julian asked.

"I'm waiting on the full financial history going back so far to come in. Basic information shows it could fund the training part-time, but not full-time. Not like the training Sophia was receiving."

Julian spun his key chain. "Was Nina linked to a man? Possibly someone with means to help her out financially?"

Brody shook his head. "There's nothing about any other man. Not much else on her at all. Her focus shifts to Sophia, who was set on the road to become an Olympian gymnast from a young age. Nina sent Sophia to gymnastics camps all over the world, finally hiring private tutors so Sophia could earn her diploma at fifteen. Sophia has trained under some of the most well-known coaches. At eighteen, she moved to Plano, Texas, to call the popular WOGA, World Olympic Gymnastics Academy, her gym."

Feeling something like an intruder, Julian laid down his key-chain as he listened to the details of Sophia's early life.

"There's nothing about Nina during this time, except her attendance at Sophia's main competitions. We do know she retired and sold her studio last year."

"She was only forty. What did she use for income?"

Brody looked up from the file. "That's why I requested a full financial history."

Julian nodded.

"Sophia won at Nationals last week and was announced to be part of the Olympic team. The girls on the team were given two weeks to report to the training gym in Huntsville. Sophia came to the Village to visit with her mother before going back to Texas. She has garnered a lot of media interest since the announcement of her making the Olympic team." Brody closed the file and tossed it into their in-box.

"I'm assuming the next item we have on Nina is her murder?"

Brody nodded. "Yes, in a nutshell."

"I think the full financial will give us a bigger picture."

"I hope so." Brody stood and grabbed his coffee mug from the corner of his desk. "Because nothing else raises a red flag." He tilted the empty cup toward Julian. "Want a cup?"

"Uh, no thanks."

Brody chuckled as he headed across the station toward the coffee area reeking of the previous night's last pot.

"Where are we on forensics?" Julian asked as soon as Brody returned.

"They finished with the quilt about fifteen minutes ago. They found a couple of stains on it, so they're running tests on them. We can pick it up, whenever we want."

"Good. I know having it will make Sophia feel better. I'll pick it up and take it to her as soon as I finish reviewing the case files."

Brody just stared at him. Said nothing, just stared.

Julian ignored him and opened the case file on the computer. Brody had already updated it with the report on Nina. Julian stared at the notes. They had precious little to build a case with. No fingerprints, no foreign DNA, except that on Nina's shirt and the DNA report wouldn't come back until tomorrow. No suspects.

"We're missing something about Nina Montgomery."

"I agree." Brody took a sip of his coffee. "I'm hoping the full financials might give us a clue."

The phone on Brody's desk rang. He leaned over and lifted it to his ear. "Brody Alexander."

A moment passed. "Yes."

Another moment. "I do. Thanks. I'm on my way." He hung up the phone.

"Well?" Julian lifted his keychain.

"Remember the neighbors who were out of town?"

Julian nodded. "Supposed to be back today."

"They got in late last night to find someone broke into their garage."

"Just the garage?" Odd. "Was a car stolen?"

Brody shook his head, smiling. "Nothing was missing, but there was one item that had been disturbed. Guess what it was."

Julian shook his head. "Amaze me."

"Their golf cart."

Julian's pulse raced. "It wasn't taken, but they could tell it was disturbed? How?"

Brody grinned. "Don't know, but they're giving their statement in robbery division right now. I'd put a notice on all surrounding addresses to notify me if anything came up."

"Well, let's go talk to them."

"I thought you'd never ask." Brody waved his arm in a mock flourish to let Julian lead the way.

The robbery division was always crowded. Luckily, since Brody had the alert set on the neighboring addresses, the officer on duty had seen the flag and put Roger and Linda Parrish in an interview room to wait for them. Julian and Brody stepped into the connecting room, and Julian nodded at the officer monitoring the couple from the mirror.

"Background on them?" Brody asked as a way of greeting.

"Roger, age fifty-four, and Linda, age fifty-two, Parrish. Roger retired from the stock market three years ago and now teaches volunteer classes every week to rehabilitated criminals at the downtown Little Rock YMCA. They live modestly on retirement and pension funds. Linda is a retired schoolteacher. They had been in Arizona visiting their only daughter and her fiancé until late last night. Neither have any priors."

"Thanks." Brody glanced at Julian. "Let's go see what's what."

The couple looked up as Brody and Julian entered the room. They looked exactly like the report presented them: a middle-aged couple living within their means. No fancy jewelry. No designer clothes. Just the appearance of a normal retired couple.

"Mr. and Mrs. Parrish. I'm Detective Frazier and this is Detective Alexander." Julian took the seat across from them. Brody leaned against the wall near the corner of the room.

"I must say, I'm a bit impressed with the attention given a break-in without anything having been taken." Roger Parrish ran a hand through his thinning salt-and-pepper hair. "I thought we'd just fill out a form and be done."

"Your case is a little special. Nothing was taken, you say, but you know someone broke in?" Julian studied Linda Parrish. She was paler than her husband—probably didn't play golf, her hair was definitely dyed because her roots were a shade lighter than her length, and a few age spots appeared on her hands.

"Yes. My wife and I left on Wednesday morning to visit our daughter in Arizona."

"She'd just gotten engaged, you see, so we wanted to surprise her. He's a nice enough young man, a little older than her, but he's handsome and he can support her well. We—"

"I don't think they care about Christi's fiancé, dear." Roger patted his wife's arm. "We always check and double-check the house before we go out of town, so I'm positive of how things were left. When we returned last night and pulled into the garage, we immediately knew someone had been in the garage and moved the golf cart."

"How can you be sure?" Brody pushed off the wall, pulled out the chair beside Julian, and sat.

Roger smiled. "I like to be able to find everything in our garage. A place for everything and everything in its place."

Linda snorted, very unladylike. "He's a control freak about his garage. The tools are hung on a pegboard with an outline so they don't get mixed up. He has outlines for everything."

Roger patted her arm again. "I have to use outlines because poor Linda here, well, she doesn't place as much importance on organization as I do. The entire place would be a wreck if she were left to her own devices, bless her heart."

"So, how are you positive the golf cart was moved?" Brody asked.

"He put markers on the garage floor to line up with the golf cart so I would know exactly where to park the cart."

"It's to ensure plenty of room for the car to fully open the driver's door and not hit it, dear."

"So, the golf cart wasn't on its marks?" Julian probed.

Roger shook his head. "No. It was a good foot off the markers. That's what made me notice it immediately, because I couldn't open the driver's door entirely."

"And you're sure it was parked correctly when you left Wednesday?" Brody asked.

"Positive. I always double-check everything before we leave town. The alarm system. The garage. We even wait to make sure the garage door is all the way down before we leave the driveway. We take the precautions." Roger nodded as he spoke.

"Alarm system? Did your alarm go off?" Julian forced himself not to let his excitement show. If the system showed an alarm going off around the time of Nina's murder, they could firm up their timeline.

"Our garage isn't part of the alarm system. It's how we know they didn't even try to get into the house. The security company said the alarm never went off, and it was still on and active when we arrived home last night."

Which meant whoever broke into the garage and borrowed the golf cart knew the couple would be gone. That took planning.

"Who all knew you were going to visit your daughter?" Julian asked.

"Oh, everybody. I'd told all my friends and neighbors about Christi's engagement." Linda smiled with pride.

"Nina Montgomery. Did you tell her?" Brody interjected.

"Why, of course. Nina was proud as punch over her Sophia's making the Olympic team and I was proud Christi had found love."

Great. So the information was general knowledge. Still, someone would have to have been ready to seize the opportunity. "How long had you been planning this visit?"

"Oh, a little less than a month. He proposed over the Memorial Day weekend," Linda said.

Plenty of time to have planned the attack, right down to the time when people wouldn't be paying attention.

"Have you touched the golf cart since you got back?" Julian asked.

Roger shook his head. "I knew right off it'd been moved, so I didn't touch it in case you needed to dust it for fingerprints." He poked his chest out like a peacock spreading his feathers. "I watch all those forensics documentaries."

Thank you, investigation channel. "You're exactly right." Julian nodded to Brody, who jumped up and left. "We're going to get a unit to go with you. They'll have to bring the golf cart back here, you understand, just to be thorough."

Julian didn't miss the frown crossing Mr. Parrish's face, so he added, "So we don't make a mess in your garage with our chemicals and equipment."

"Oh. I understand." Roger nodded.

"Another question, if I might. How well do you know Nina Montgomery?"

Linda crossed her arms over her chest. "She's nice enough. She gave our daughter some dance lessons years ago, but said Christi's heart wasn't into becoming a professional dancer."

Roger shifted in his chair. "We saw the policeman at her gate and wondered if maybe her home had been broken into as well." He raised his bushy eyebrows.

Julian didn't miss Linda's perking up. He recognized the signs of someone who not only liked to be in the know, but to let others know she was in the know. Better to let her squelch talk of anything else . . . "Yes, Mrs. Montgomery's house was broken into as well last week."

"Oh, my goodness." Linda pressed her hand against her chest. "Was anything stolen?"

"We're working on that. Do you know of any problems Nina might have with anyone?" It was a long shot, but Julian would exhaust every lead he could find.

"I'm not aware of anything, but she had been getting a lot of attention since Sophia came home to visit. With her making the Olympic team and all."

Julian nodded. He knew it'd been reaching, but still . . . he'd hoped.

Brody stepped back into the room. "An officer is ready to escort you home and impound your golf cart."

Julian stood and shook the couple's hands. "Thank you both so much. We'll make sure to get your golf cart back to you as soon as we can."

An officer led them away.

"Sophia said they wore gloves, so there probably aren't any prints." Julian headed back toward their work stations.

"Maybe. We've seen people forget to put on gloves at the worst times. Maybe we'll get lucky."

"Maybe. Or maybe they left some DNA or something in the cart."

"I'll request a rush," Brody said as he plopped down behind his desk.

"I'm going to grab the quilt and head over to the hospital. Maybe Sophia's remembered something new."

Brody grinned and shook his head.

"What?"

Brody just kept shaking his head. "Nothing, man."

Julian didn't want to have this discussion anyway. "Okay. Call me if you find out anything." He headed toward the evidence room, his step a little lighter.

Why he got excited over the idea of seeing Sophia, he wasn't sure. He wasn't even sure if he liked the idea.

10

Oh . . . mercy. She could frighten children with how scary she looked.

Sophia blinked and stared at her reflection in the mirror over the sink in her new hospital room's bathroom. It was the first time she had been able to see the damage done to her face.

She looked like Frankenstein. Three long cuts, two on her forehead and one along the top of her left cheekbone, held rows of stitches. Both her eyes had been blackened and the bruising was now a deep purple. Her right eye even had the lovely yellow-brown extending up into her eyebrow. Her lip had been busted, and now, the scab was bigger than the largest cold sore known to man.

Yep, she looked like Frankenstein.

"You okay in there?" Charlie called out.

She knocked on the door, hoping Charlie would realize that meant she was fine. Well, that was quite an overstatement.

Sophia stared at her reflection again. *God, please. I didn't think I was vain, but this . . . oh, Lord.* Tears filled her eyes, but she swiped them away with the back of her hand. She jerked off the gloves and tossed them in the trash, then touched her face with the only exposed part of her hands—her fingertips. When the nurse had changed her dressings last night, she'd left the tips of Sophia's fingers exposed. At least she had feeling in her fingertips.

She blinked a final time before opening the bathroom door.

"Ready to get back in bed now?" Charlie held Sophia's arm, taking on most of her weight.

Sophia nodded and let Charlie help her back into the hospital bed. After being moved to a new room and having been fed a breakfast of juice and Jell-O, she'd felt more energized than ever. As soon as Charlie had come, she'd gotten the nurse's approval to get up and about. After just three laps around the larger hospital room, Sophia was drained. A row of sweat beads dotted her upper lip.

It felt good to be doing something physical again. Not too surprising since her body was used to strenuous workouts daily. Even if she could never do mat work again, she needed to stay in shape. She always had, even as a little girl, stretched with her mother and worked out in the dance studio.

She pushed away the grief threatening to cripple her as she realized she'd never get to see *Mamochka* pirouette again. Or hug her. Or hear her voice.

Sophia let out a heavy sigh and leaned back against the pillows. Charlie helped straighten the covers over her. "There. All better."

A light knock sounded.

"Ms. Montgomery," a doctor said as he entered. No nurse trailed his steps carrying a chart. His gaze fixed on Charlie sitting beside the bed. "Oh, I'm sorry. I didn't realize you had visitors. I'll come back later."

"No, Charlie's my translator, since I still can't speak."

He stopped and turned back to Sophia. "Interesting," he said, almost under his breath. "It's fine. I'll be back later."

"But she can translate what I need to say."

He rushed from the room without a response.

Frustration clawed up Sophia's spine. Who was this doctor? Or was he a lab technician? Their white coats all looked the same to her.

"Want me to chase him down?" Charlie asked.

Sophia shook her head and mouthed, "Probably wouldn't do any good anyway. The only doctor who seems to be able to give me any information is Dr. Rhoads. I haven't even seen my hand surgeon." The idea flitted across her mind. "You don't think it was him, do you?" Lord, she hoped not, because he didn't exactly exude confidence.

"I don't know. I can go ask if you want." Charlie stood.

"No. If it's him, he'll be back later, like he said." Still, his behavior was odd. And wouldn't every doctor who looked at her chart realize she couldn't speak? Had he even bothered to read her chart?

"So, do you want some water?" Charlie lifted the big insulated cup on the bedside table.

"Please. You'd think I was dehydrated or something."

Charlie eased the straw between her lips. "Well, you did exert yourself walking around."

The cold water felt smooth all the way down Sophia's throat. Refreshing. She'd never realized how good water actually tasted. Or maybe she was just starting to appreciate the little things.

Charlie pulled the straw back and a drop of water dribbled down Sophia's chin. "Oops." She grabbed a tissue from the box on the table and patted away the wetness. "There. Sorry."

"It's okay. I'm surprised Julian didn't spill any broth on me last night."

Charlie leaned her hip against the side rail of the bed. "Julian fed you last night?"

Heat spread all across Sophia's face and neck, and she dropped her gaze to the bed sheet. "Well, it was kinda by accident," she mouthed.

Charlie bent over and put her face where Sophia could see it. "I can't read your lips if I can't see your mouth."

"Sorry." Sophia straightened. "It wasn't intentional. They brought me the broth, then left before Julian could protest, and I was so hungry my stomach growled, and then when I smelled it, my stomach growled even louder and Julian felt sorry for me . . ."

Charlie grinned. "Hey, don't run out of breath explaining it to me, girl."

Heat flamed in Sophia's face, but she managed to keep her head upright.

"Hey, I'm just teasing you."

"I know." But her face continued to burn.

"Oh," Charlie whispered. "I see."

Embarrassment spread throughout Sophia's stomach. "Is it that obvious?" she mouthed.

"Sophia." Charlie eased into the chair. "Julian's a great guy, don't get me wrong. I like him."

"But?"

"But you are a victim in a case he's working. It's natural for you to view him as a hero and feel some sort of attraction to him."

"I know." Sophia felt even more miserable. She knew Charlie was right, but it didn't stop her feelings.

"Hey." Charlie touched Sophia's leg to get her attention. "It's okay. Nothing to be embarrassed about. Your secret is safe with me, okay?"

"Thanks." Sophia smiled.

A knock sounded, then Julian poked his head around the corner. "Okay to come in?"

"Sure," Charlie answered. "We're just talking about how your feeding ability last night was better than mine."

"Oh." There was an unmistakable uncertainty tone to his voice.

Charlie laughed. "I spilled water on her. Guess I need to work on my bedside manner."

"Well, I come bearing gifts." Julian did, in fact, walk in with a stuffed plastic garbage bag in tow.

"Presents?" Charlie looked from Julian to Sophia, then back to Julian.

Sophia's heart pounded. And pounded. And pounded. Even as heat flushed to her cheeks. The cheeks she knew were swollen and cut.

Julian opened the bag and pulled out her mother's quilt, and all concerns about how monsterish she looked disappeared. He spread the quilt over the bed.

Sophia didn't fight the tears as she ran her fingertips over the familiar material, letting the memories run through her . . .

"Mamochka, what's this costume from?"

"Ah, that, my sweet, was when I danced as Slyph in La Sylphide.*"*

Sophia touched the white, gauzy bodice. "It's beautiful. I bet you made Slyph beautiful."

"A sylph is a mythical creature, beautiful already because it doesn't really exist." Laughing, Mamochka *planted a kiss atop Sophia's head. "The ballet itself is actually a sad story of a man named James who chases after a mythical creature, leaving his fiancée at the altar. He ends up trapping the sylph, but it kills her. Then he watches his fiancée marry his best friend, so he is left all alone."*

"How sad." Sophia stared at the quilt square made with the white material. "What happened to your James, Mamochka*?"*

"My James? Oh, you mean the man who danced with me in the ballet?"

Sophia nodded.

Mamochka *frowned. "Dimitri chased what he couldn't have, too, and ended up alone." She shook her head. "It doesn't matter. Your father, now HE was a true hero, and beautiful in every way."*

"It's breathtaking," Charlie whispered almost reverently, pulling Sophia back to the present.

"Yes, it is," Sophia mouthed. "Thank you, Julian, for bringing it to me."

"I told you I'd bring it to you." She didn't miss the hue of red filling his face.

From the expression on Charlie's face, she hadn't missed it either.

"I don't know what got on it there," he pointed to the large stain on the center, focal point of the quilt, the whole Sugar Plum Fairy costume.

"Oh, it's always been there." *Mamochka* had always told her the red stain represented the blood of every ballet dancer. "I think it was a soda or something."

"Well, forensics extracted some of it and is running tests. It's just policy."

Charlie's eyes feasted on the quilt. She ran her hand over one of the corner squares with pink satin material. "This is exquisite."

Sophia smiled and nodded. "It's from when she danced as Medora in *Le Corsaire*." She closed her eyes and remembered the story. "*Mamochka* was seventeen and had just graduated and been accepted to the New York City Ballet Company. She'd earned her soloist rank after dancing the title role in *Raymonda,* but she wasn't content to be one among so many. The role of Medora gave her the opportunity to shine."

Sophia opened her eyes and met Charlie's intense stare. "Do you know the story of *Le Corsaire?*"

Charlie shook her head, slowly, as if mesmerized.

Sophia glanced at Julian on the other side of her bed. He, too, looked spellbound.

"Well, it's loosely based on the poem, *The Corsair,* by Lord Byron."

"Oh. I know the poem," Charlie said. "The ballet is about the poem? I have to admit, I was always attracted to Conrad."

Sophia nodded. "He was quite the noble character. I loved the poem. My mother said after she'd danced as Medora, it allowed her to join the rank of the principals with the company."

"I bet. I'd love to see that ballet."

Sophia gave her a smile, then turned to Julian. "Thank you so much for bringing this to me. It means a lot." Her stomach tightened as she fought to remember Charlie's admonishment.

She was just a victim in the case he was working.

Nothing more.

———

Her smile made his adrenaline rush as though he'd just run a hundred-yard dash. "You're quite welcome." No, he needed to stay on a business level. He was the detective on her mother's murder case.

Julian cleared his throat. "I do have a couple of questions for you." He pulled his notebook from his pocket.

"Go ahead," she mouthed and Charlie said.

"Do you know a Roger and Linda Parrish?"

She nodded. "They're my mother's neighbors. I don't really *know them* know them. I know their daughter, Christi, better. She's a few years older than me. She took dance lessons from *Mamochka* at the studio. Why?"

"We're just following up on some leads."

"Do you think they're involved in this?" Sophia shook her head. "Mrs. Parrish is a bit of a gossip, but they're nice people. I remember Mr. Parrish came over to fix our kitchen sink one night when a gasket blew and water spewed out everywhere. We couldn't get the water to stop and it was after five. She called Mr. Parrish and he came right over. Turned off the water to the tap so we could wait until morning to call the plumber. Nice man."

He could tell she was agitated about the possibility of the couple being involved. "They were out of town on Thursday night." Although, the police were checking their alibi, just to be thorough.

"Oh. Good. I mean, not good, but I can tell you, Roger Parrish was not one of the men who attacked me and my mother."

"I understand. However, we do believe Roger Parrish's golf cart was the means the attackers used to arrive at your place undetected." Using the golf cart meant easier access, and they returned it, believing no one would ever know it'd been used.

And just when her face had begun to show more natural color and not the pallor of illness, he had to tell her more things that made her pale by the second.

"What do you mean?"

"It means he came forward with the information that someone had used his golf cart, then put it back, assuming he wouldn't notice it'd been used, while he was out of town."

Sophia laughed. "Mr. Parrish would notice if a leaf on his rosebushes in the front flowerbed had been touched. I remember Christi used to complain he was obsessed with organization."

It was nice to see her smile back. "Well, it's serving us well he's so obsessed. Had he not noticed his golf cart had been moved, we might not have ever known how they arrived at your place."

Her smile slid off her face.

Positive, Frazier. Be more positive.

"We are impounding it as we speak to have forensics go over it with a fine-tooth comb. We're hopeful we can find something to reveal the identity of the attackers."

"Hope*ful* or hop*ing*?" Charlie crinkled her nose. "The emphasis was from her, too."

"I figured." He met Sophia's stare head-on.

And was nearly undone by the raw grief shimmering in her eyes. She looked so fragile, yet he knew she was such a strong young woman . . .

"It's okay. I know you're doing everything you can."

He'd find who was responsible. He would not let her down.

"Hey, at least he doesn't run off like your doctor," Charlie laughed to Sophia, who grinned.

Julian shot Charlie a quizzical look.

"Earlier, a doctor came in to see Sophia. He saw me, said he didn't realize she had company and would come back later, and ran away." She grinned wider at Sophia. "Maybe I scared him off."

It didn't sound right. "Which doctor was this?" he asked.

Sophia shrugged. "I don't know. I'd never seen him before. I thought he might be my hand surgeon. Although . . ."

Julian's gut clenched. "Although what?"

"Well, he seemed surprised I couldn't speak. I would have thought my surgeon who is supposed to be reading my chart every day would know that." She shrugged again. "Or maybe he thought I should've made quicker progress with my vocal chords healing."

"When was this? About what time did he come by?" The clenching in Julian's gut intensified.

Sophia and Charlie locked stares. "About an hour to an hour and half ago, maybe?"

"Hang on, I'll be right back." He rushed from the room, storming to the nurses' station. He pulled his badge. "Right now, I need to know what doctors have been on this floor in the last two hours."

"Uh . . . let me get the charge nurse for you, sir," the young, wide-eyed, ponytailed, blonde nurse stammered.

"Please hurry and get her." He pushed away from the counter and glanced up and down the hall.

He marched to the officer stationed outside Sophia's room. "About an hour and a half ago, a doctor came into the room and left quickly."

The officer nodded. "Yes, sir."

"Who was he?"

"I-I don't know, sir. He hadn't been in to see her before."

"And you just let him in?" What was wrong with this uniform? Didn't he realize there was a reason he was stationed outside her room?

"Sir, he wore one of the doctors' white coats and had a hospital ID badge on."

"Did you catch the name on the badge?"

"No, sir."

Great. It could've belonged to a janitor for all they knew. The young uniformed officer looked like he'd been called to the principal's office.

In a way, he had. He should have documented every person's name who came into Sophia's room. Her mother had been murdered, and she'd been left for dead. If they'd found out she was still alive . . . her life was at stake.

"I was told you wanted to see me," a woman's voice drew his attention back down the hall.

Julian pointed at the officer. "I'll discuss this in more detail with you in just a few minutes." He headed to the nurses' station. "Yes." He flashed his badge again. "I need a list of every doctor who's been on this floor over the last two hours."

"I can tell you which ones have made rounds. I can tell you who has checked in, but we have no way to keep track of every single doctor's whereabouts in a hospital this size."

Julian glanced at the half-globe on the ceiling. He pointed at it. "Is that a security camera?"

The charge nurse followed his point. "Yes."

"Thank you." Julian rushed back to Sophia's room. He took a deep breath before he stepped inside.

"Julian, what's going on?" Sophia mouthed, her face pale again. Charlie didn't look much better.

"I'm just checking on a few things. I'll be back soon." He turned to leave.

Charlie grabbed his arm just as he reached the door. "Julian."

"I don't know," he whispered, knowing the question. "I'm going to look and see if I can see who it was on the security cameras."

"You don't think it was a doctor?"

"I need to check it."

"But you don't think it was?"

"Doctors don't usually adjust their rounds around a patient visiting, and they surely don't run off." He squeezed her arm. "Stay with her, please. I'll be back soon."

Charlie nodded, then headed back to Sophia's bedside.

Julian shut her door. "Officer, no one is to go in this room unless you call me and get approval, do you understand?" He wrote down his cell number on a piece of paper in his notebook, tore it out, and handed it to the officer. "No one except me or Detective Alexander unless you call me. Got it?"

"Yes, sir."

Julian turned and headed toward the elevators, adrenaline pushing his steps faster and faster. This could be a big break in the case.

Or it could be nothing.

As he stepped into the elevator and pushed the button for the security office floor, one thought slammed against him: how did they know she was still alive?

11

He thinks the doctor . . . the man, is one of them, doesn't he?" Sophia mouthed to Charlie. "Julian thinks he came here to kill me, doesn't he?"

"He's just being cautious and thorough. It's his job."

Sophia narrowed her eyes. "Don't lie to me, Charlie."

Charlie sighed and slumped into the chair. "I'm sorry. He is being cautious and thorough, but yes, he's suspicious of the man who came in here. He believes he isn't a doctor, but won't panic us until he's checked."

Sophia's heart pounded. Good thing she wasn't still hooked up to the beeping machine because it would be going overtime right now.

"It's going to be okay. Don't get all sideways on me now." Charlie made direct eye contact with her.

"I'm fine. A little unnerved is all." Then she remembered she was never alone. "God's got this anyway, right?"

Charlie smiled. "Right, and we might be making a big deal out of nothing. It's entirely possible the guy was legit and just strange."

"Yeah. I know." Yet the more she thought about it, the more she realized that probably wasn't true. The guy had come here . . . for her. She closed her eyes and tried to remember what he looked like.

She opened her eyes and mouthed to Charlie, "We need to remember what he looks like. Julian will definitely want to know as many details as possible."

"Right." Charlie grabbed a pen and piece of paper from her purse. "I'd say he was almost six feet."

Sophia nodded. "Maybe weighed one-eighty or one-ninety?"

"Yeah, I'd say that's about right. He had light brown hair, but I didn't see any blond in it. Did you?"

"No." And now, with his image in her mind, it bugged her. "Charlie, he didn't look intimidating at all."

Charlie broke eye contact to stare at her notes, then looked back at her. "You're right. He didn't."

"Don't you think the person those attackers would send to finish me off would at least look a little intimidating or scary?"

Charlie nodded. "I do. He didn't look like either."

"Now that I think about it, he looked like he was a little scared." The wideness of his eyes when he saw Charlie, who was, by no stretch of the imagination, intimidating or scary. The way he rushed out . . . "I don't think he was with the men who attacked me and *Mamochka*. He just doesn't look the part, nor did he act threatening in any way."

"I agree, but he didn't seem like a doctor either."

"Maybe he's new? Or one of the doctors in training or something."

"Could be." Either way, they'd have to wait until Julian got back to discuss it with him. Sophia breathed a little easier now that she'd thought it through and didn't think the guy was out to harm her. He had probably—

"I'm sorry, but I can't let you in unless I get permission," the officer's voice outside rose.

Charlie stood. "I'll go check it out." She disappeared out the door, then returned moments later, carrying Sophia's lunch tray.

Sophia laughed.

"Julian told the officer no one but he and Brody could come in without his permission. The poor guy was trying to call Julian's cell and block the aide from bringing the tray at the same time. I thought I'd save the poor guy." She set the tray on the table and lifted the lid. "Oh, look. Yummy beef broth, yogurt, and chocolate milk."

Actually, it sounded really, really good. Maybe being scared for your life, then being relieved made you hungry. Either way, Sophia was famished.

"Hmm." Charlie looked at Sophia's hands, then darted her gaze around the room. "I know you hate to depend on others, and I'm more than willing to feed you, but I have an idea to help you feed yourself. Interested?"

It would be awesome to not have to have someone feed her. It was humiliating. She nodded.

"The broth's too thin for this, so I'll just let you drink it out of a straw when it cools a little, okay?"

Sophia nodded.

"Same with the milk." Charlie rolled her eyes. "Well, with the straw, I mean. It's obviously not too hot." She took the top off the yogurt and set it on the tray, then went to the bathroom, returning with one of the pairs of disposable gloves. "Okay, let's glove you up."

After the gloves were secure, Charlie pulled open one of the drawers and grabbed a roll of self-adhering elastic wrap. She situated the spoon in Sophia's right hand and then slowly and gently wrapped the bandage around, securing the spoon to Sophia's hand. "There."

Charlie adjusted the height of the table, then arranged the tray and yogurt cup so Sophia could manipulate the cup with just the fingertips on her left hand. Charlie put the napkin over Sophia's chest. "You might make a little mess. It's okay if you do." She stepped back. "Go ahead and give it a try."

Sophia took a deep breath, then tried.

And failed.

God, please. I'm not asking to win a gold, just to be able to feed myself.

It took her three times, but she finally got the spoon into the cup, and was able to get it into her mouth. And she didn't even spill a drop!

"Yeah, you're awesome," Charlie said.

Sophia made quick work of the yogurt.

"Well, look at you." Charlie helped her scrape the last bite, then undid her hands. "The broth is cool enough now. Would you like some?"

Sophia nodded, and Charlie put the straw to her lips.

She'd just finished off her milk when Julian returned. "I just reviewed all the video footage from the last two and a half hours on your floor. I saw the man enter and leave three minutes later, but we didn't get a clear image of his face, so we have no identification."

"Tell him what we discussed," Sophia mouthed to Charlie.

Nodding, Charlie filled Julian in on their impressions. When she was finished, Julian stared at Sophia. "You weren't apprehensive about him?"

She shook her head. "Besides, God's with me. I have to believe I didn't die for a reason. I'm not going to start being scared now."

"Hmm. I stopped by the nurses' station again and had them check your chart. No doctor or nurse or therapist or lab technician had any notation of coming by, or intent to come by and see you today. And before you say anything, I checked with the floor's charge nurse about what your hand doctor looks like. He's in his early fifties and balding, nothing like the description you two came up with."

"Then I have no idea who he was, but I truly don't believe he's with the men who attacked me and my mother. He seemed more like . . . well, like a weasel than an aggressor."

Julian chuckled. "A weasel, huh?"

It did strange things to Sophia's heart to see him laugh. She could almost imagine him out of his profession, laughing. With her.

Heat infused her face and she shot a glance at Charlie, who met her stare with a raised eyebrow.

It was almost as if Charlie could read her mind. How was it possible, to have someone know her so intimately, when she'd only known her for such a short time? She'd been on teams and in training with girls all her life, but she'd never bonded with any of them. Was it only because of the brutality of the attack on her that she was more readable? Or the grief from losing her mother?

Julian kept smiling. "I did, however, learn your hand doctor is supposed to make rounds soon. He's actually finishing up a surgery, then the nurse said he'll make rounds. And yes, I asked . . . he's scheduled to actually come talk to you today, instead of just reading your chart."

If Sophia could talk, she'd sing a halleluiah chorus right now.

"Thought that might make you happy." Julian glanced around the room. "Much nicer digs than before. More spacious."

Sophia smiled, then caught Charlie staring at Julian as if he'd just sprouted another head. Was she reading his mind, too? Julian stared back at Charlie, and it was as if they were having a full conversation between them with not a single word said.

Finally, Julian cleared his throat and looked back at Sophia. "The officer outside will be checking ID badges from this point forward. Verifying everyone who comes into the room."

"I hope you told the poor guy he could let the aides bring in meal trays. If I hadn't intervened and gotten Sophia's lunch tray, she'd have died of starvation," Charlie teased.

"He should be thorough."

"Don't you intimidate him, Julian Frazier. I know what a bully you can be," Charlie said.

"I'm not a bully. I'm just making sure he's doing his job." Julian's Adam's apple bobbed. "But, I need to get back to the station. Brody called, and they're going over the golf cart now. I want to be there in case they find anything." He smiled at Sophia, and her mouth formed a returning smile on its own accord. "I'll be back later this evening. If you need me in the meantime, Charlie knows my number."

Charlie stood. "I do." She smiled at Sophia. "I'm going to grab a bite and let you rest for a bit. I'll be back in less than an hour."

"Thank you." Sophia watched them leave.

Once they'd closed the door, she closed her eyes and let her fingers caress another square on her mother's quilt, the deep, red from *Mamochka's* portrayal of Death in *La Valse.*

"Why weren't you the girl in white?" Sophia asked, watching her mother sew the intricate pattern with the dark crimson bodice material.

Mamochka *laughed, the sound as light and graceful as she was when dancing. "Oh, my sweet. I've always liked dancing the passionate roles of the dark. Like the dark swan in* Swan Lake. *And Death in* La Valse.*"*

"But you're too pretty to be mean."

She set down her needle and thread and hugged Sophia. "You, my dear, are an angel."

Sophia ran her hand over the tulle of the skirt, then reached for the stack of playbills. She flipped through them, staring at her mother's pictures. So beautiful. "No, Mamochka, you're the angel."

"What do you think you're doing?"

Julian strode down the hospital hallway, Charlie dogging his every step. She grabbed his arm and spun him to face her. "Julian. What are you doing?"

"I'm working a case."

"That's not what I meant, and you know it." Charlie crossed her arms over her chest.

No, he knew what she meant, but he didn't want to discuss it with her right now. Maybe never, but at least not until he got some grasp on exactly what this odd sense of attraction and protection he felt about Sophia.

"I see the way you look at her."

"Mind your own business, Charlie."

"You saved her, Julian. The girl's got hero-worship in her eyes every time she looks at you. Don't you dare bat those dark-as-night eyes at her to get information for your case, then break her heart. She's not used to men like you."

"Men like me?" What, was he some kind of player or something? Seriously, he rarely dated.

"Yes, men like you. Men." Charlie shook her head and let out a heavy sigh. "Don't you see? Sophia's been so sheltered, so wrapped up in her gymnastics and training, I bet she's never even so much as been kissed by someone over the age of twenty-one."

"I'm not kissing her, Charlie." But if he was honest with himself, he'd admit he wanted to. Desperately. Last night when he'd been feeding her, he'd been so sorely tempted to just lightly graze his lips against hers.

"Be sure you don't, Julian. I mean it. That girl in there is a good girl, and she's been through a lot. She's lost everything."

"I know, Charlie." He didn't need her telling him how to act, what to do, or how to feel. "This is my case. I know exactly what she's been through and what she's lost. You don't have to remind me of that."

"I just don't want to see her get hurt again is all. I like her. I care about her."

Problem was, so did he. "I've got to get back to the station. Are you staying for a while?"

"Yeah. At least until her hand doctor comes by. She has a lot of questions for him."

"I would imagine. I'll check back later." He turned and left.

The afternoon sun beat down on the parking lot, making it downright sweltering. Soon, the Fourth of July celebrations would begin, and there'd be even more going on in the village. He hoped to solve Sophia's case before then.

He met Brody back at the station, down in the forensics lab where the technicians had already started working on the golf cart.

"Anything new with Sophia?" Brody asked.

Julian nodded, filling him in on the strange man who'd posed as a doctor and gotten into her room, ending with, "Sophia and Charlie both said the man didn't appear aggressive in any way, I let the officer at the door understand how important it is to verify those ID badges."

Brody nodded. "Now might be a good time to send the sketch artist over to the hospital. I know you wanted to wait on Sophia to get a little better to work with the artist on sketches of the men who attacked her, but I don't think we can wait any longer. And while the artist's there, he can make a sketch of the fake doctor."

"Yeah."

"Great. I'll call the artist."

"Will you call Charlie and let her know as well?" He didn't want to hear another lecture from her.

"Sure." Brody stepped out of the observation room, already lifting his phone to his ear.

The head forensics tech waved at Julian to come to the intercom. Julian did and pressed the button. "Whatcha got, Robert?"

"No fingerprints, but we found two areas we're extracting DNA to test. Found four hairs, too."

"Let me know as soon as you get the results, okay? Thanks for rushing this."

Robert gave a curt nod, then went back into the lab area. Julian met Brody in the hall and filled him in.

"Let's just pray there's evidence to not only identify the attackers, but link the golf cart to the crime." Brody slipped his phone back into his hip holder.

"I'm hoping the same myself, partner."

"Yeah, but I'm *praying.*" Brody chuckled.

Julian remained silent as they walked back to their desks. Even after everything Sophia had gone through, she still clung to her faith. He normally would chock it up to her age and naïveté, but Brody was by no means young or naïve. Maybe they were onto something.

No. He'd chased down that rabbit hole before, only to have Eli cut down in front of him. Eli had loved the Lord, and God didn't save him.

If God wouldn't save a good man like Eli, there was no hope for Julian.

12

Your fingers aren't broken at all, and your surgery site is healing nicely with no sign of infection. I'm going to order less bandaging to give you more range of motion. No grabbing things yet, though. You can't bend your knuckles like usual. Just your fingers. Understand?" Dr. Davies, the hand surgeon, pushed his glasses back up the bridge of his hawklike nose.

Sophia nodded. The doctor had examined her hands carefully, cleaned the area himself, then rewrapped them in a much looser, thinner manner. She looked at Charlie and mouthed the question burning her heart. "Will I ever be able to compete as a gymnast again?"

Charlie's voice trailed off.

Dr. Davies slowly shook his head. "I'm sorry. I'm a great surgeon and this was clean breaks with textbook repairs, but the extensiveness of the damage . . . I doubt you'll be able to put your entire body weight on just your hands again."

Sophia pressed her lips together and nodded. Everything got a little blurry as her eyes filled with tears.

"I'm sorry." Dr. Davies patted her shoulder, then took her chart and left.

The tears wouldn't be denied. They slipped down her face in silence.

"I'm so sorry, Sophia," Charlie said, her voice cracking.

Sophia sniffled and wiped tears onto her shoulder. *Lord, You have to help me. I'm not strong enough to bear this on my own. Please show me the path You want me to take.*

The officer stuck his head into the room. "Ms. Montgomery?"

"Yes?" Charlie answered.

"Your gr—Alena Borin is here to see you."

Charlie looked at Sophia. "Your call."

She'd just gotten the most devastating news . . . she didn't know if she could handle seeing the woman who never wanted her born.

Forgive.

The word reverberated in her mind. Over and over.

Forgive. Forgive. Forgive.

"Sophia?"

Hard as it would be, she knew what she had to do. She nodded at Charlie.

"Yes, it's okay. Send her in," Charlie told the guard. "Are you sure?" she whispered to Sophia.

"No, but it's what I need to do." *With Your strength, Jesus. Your strength.*

Alena walked into the room. "*MIlaya Moyna*, you are looking better." She stopped when she saw Charlie.

"I'm Charlie, remember? I translate for Sophia."

"You can still not talk?" Alena moved closer to the bed.

Sophia shook her head. She'd been dying to try to just say one word, but Dr. Rhoads hadn't cleared her yet and had told her not to try. She could permanently damage her vocal chords. Considering everything else she'd lost, she wasn't willing to take the chance.

"I am sor—" Her eyes widened as she stared at the quilt. "What is this?"

Oh, right. Alena was a quilter. Something good, at least one thing, had been passed down from mother to daughter to daughter. "*Mamochka* took her ballet costumes and quilted them into this. She would tell me the stories of each of the ballets as we quilted." So many wonderful, wonderful memories Sophia would hold dear to her heart forever.

"May I?" Alena held her hand over the quilt, waiting for Sophia's approval before she touched it.

Sophia nodded.

She touched the first piece, the scarlet with polka dots costume in the bottom corner. "I remember this one. Your *mamochka* was only eleven years old when she wore this." Alena's smile widened. "The Little Radish. Everyone says she is too young to dance such an important role in *Cipollino*, but she show them all. She was beautiful, even with the silly headpiece."

Sophia smiled as well. "This was back in Russia?"

"*Da*. She was studying dance at the Vaganova Ballet Academy in St. Petersburg. Everyone was surprised when she landed the role, but she was perfection on stage."

"I remember she told me that she'd been so nervous before she went on, but as soon as she entered stage right, it was as if she were dancing alone."

Alena nodded, a faraway smile on her face. "She loved to dance and dancing loved her."

Silence filled the room, but not uncomfortably so.

Alena moved her hands up to the next square, gently stroking the gauzy blue-teal material. "I remember this as well. The role made her a star in Kirov Academy here in United States."

"The Sea Princess costume," Sophia recalled.

"From *The Little Humpbacked Horse*. She was just twelve, but just like in Mother Russia, she stunned everyone with her dance maturity." Alena shook her head. "She did not dance, *MIlaya Moyna,* she floated. Everyone say so."

"What was she like? As a young girl, I mean." *Mamochka* had shared a lot of her youth and life, but Sophia hadn't an idea of what she was really like. As a person.

"She was dancer. Beautiful. Graceful."

"No, I mean what was she like as a person, not a dancer."

Alena's brows scrunched. "Dancer is who she was."

"What kind of books did she like as a girl? What did she like to do? What kind of music did she like?"

"What kind of questions are these? She liked to dance. She listened to ballet scores. She read *Dance Magazine*."

Had she not been allowed to be a person, too? Only a dancer? If so, no wonder *Mamochka* hadn't talked much about her childhood.

"Oh, I remember this ballet." Alena touched the gold and white bodice. "*Raymonda*. She was only seventeen. With her new company."

"New York City Ballet."

"*Da*. She was so beautiful. Everyone say so. Especially Dimitri. I always say he fall in love with her during this ballet."

"Dimitri?" Sophia's curiosity was piqued. She'd heard her mother mention the name a few times, but always with a scowl or frown attached to the comment.

"He loved her so. Broke his heart, she did."

"Whatever happened to him?" She didn't understand why she was curious, but she was.

"He continued to dance after my Nina, mostly with Nadia. He and Nadia were a couple for a while. After she was gone, he became financial supporter of ballet company. His family has money, always did. Another reason I thought she should stay with Dimitri."

"What about now?"

"I do not know. After my Nina stopped dancing, I did not follow the ballet. It hurt too much."

Sophia swallowed the retort burning her tongue to be released. Forgive. Forgive.

"*Mamochka* told me this was one of her favorite ballets." Sophia changed the subject, pointing to a square on the side closer to her, the satiny, deep red material. "Nikiya in *The Temple Dancer.* Do you remember it?"

Alena nodded. "The name of the ballet was actually Petipa's *La Bayadère.* Nina loved the ballet because of this costume. Pants." She shook her head, smiling. "I was shocked when I saw the costume, but as soon as she was on stage, I knew it was as perfect as she was. Stunning. Drew attention from everyone. Even Nadia, her friend and competition, said Nina *was* Nikiya."

"Nadia. I don't think I ever heard *Mamochka* mention her, but you say she was her best friend?"

"*Da. Da.* They met in New York company. Both new. Both good dancers, but Nina better. Nina knew it. So did Nadia. But Nadia has ties to Mother Russia, too, so they get friends. They go to studio together. To rehearsals together. They giggle together at home."

Sophia couldn't imagine why she'd never heard her mother mention Nadia's name once. "I've never heard of her. What's her last name?"

"Paley. Nadia Paley. You must have just forgot hearing Nina talk about her."

"No, I'm quite positive *Mamochka* never mentioned her. She never mentioned any friends from her ballet company."

"Really? But she make Nadia last costume the centerpiece of this quilt." Alena pointed to the Sugar Plum Fairy full front of the costume in the center of the quilt.

Sophia shook her head. "No, that's *Mamochka's.*"

Alena shook her head, more vehemently. "No, it is Nadia's. Nina would never have danced a role as low as a sugar plum fairy . . . she was Clara."

Sophia opened her mouth to argue, then clamped it shut. She racked her memories. Every time she and her mother had worked on the quilt, or *Mamochka* had told her stories, she'd always pointed out the centerpiece was the Sugar Plum Fairy costume from the *Nutcracker* ballet, but she'd never actually said she'd danced the part. Was it possible what Alena said was true and *Mamochka* had used her best friend's costume as the centerpiece as some sort of way of honoring her?

Alena had, as far as Sophia knew, never lied to her. Been blunt and hurtful, but honest.

Unlike *Mamochka*, so Sophia now knew.

"What happened to Nadia? Is she still performing?" Her mother had continued to follow the ballet industry news, even though she refused to take Sophia to a real ballet, only allowing Sophia to attend her own dance studio's recitals and productions.

"*Ne.* She died some time ago, *MIlaya Moyna.*"

Even younger than *Mamochka*. Too young to die. "What happened?"

"She murdered. Backstage at ballet." Alena nodded at the Sugar Plum Fairy costume. "That ballet."

⁓

"I bet I know who was your fake doctor," Brody announced as his way of greeting early Tuesday morning.

"Do tell," Julian said, turning from the open case file on the computer.

Brody tossed the morning paper down on his desk. "Seems a reporter received a tip from an *unnamed source* that newly named Olympic gymnastics team member, Sophia Montgomery, was attacked in her mother's home last week and is recovering in the hospital, following an early-morning emergency surgery."

Julian actually felt the blood drain from his face. "No."

Brody nodded. "It gets worse. He reports she's unable to speak and barely walking. Two nationals picked it up not even fifteen minutes ago."

"We have to get to the hospital. Now." Julian jumped to his feet and snatched the paper from the desk. "I'll call Charlie now and have her meet us there."

"I'll drive so you can read and get caught up." Brody led the way. "I already called the hospital and gave the word there is to be no confirmation given. I told our officer at her door to be ready." He started the car and squealed out of the station's lot, then drove in silence while Julian read.

"I want to question this . . . this . . ." he squinted to read the byline. "Carl Oxford."

"Already have the uniforms bringing him in for questioning." Brody steered the car into the hospital's parking lot.

"At least he doesn't know her mother died."

"She's not the story." Brody shut the door and hit the button on the remote to lock. "An Olympic team member attacked and the rest is the story."

Julian balled his hands into tight fists at his side as they entered the hospital. A throng of people filled the lobby, most of them with cameras and microphones.

"I'm sorry, but you can't bring your equipment in here," the poor woman in a suit tried to address them. Security officers blocked the elevators. "You'll have to wait outside. This is private property. If you don't leave the premises, I'll call the police."

"But we know Sophia Montgomery is here."

"Just tell us what floor she's on."

"Can you give us an update on her condition?"

Julian ground his teeth.

"Please. You must leave."

Nodding at Brody, Julian pulled his badge and held it up. "Police. You heard the lady, get out of the building."

Brody did the same on his side of the room. "Come on, move out."

Within minutes, the press had been escorted from the hospital.

"Thank you," the woman said.

"Ma'am, we're calling in a few uniformed officers to keep an eye on the front door, but you need to alert your security department and have more stationed at elevators and stairways," Julian told her even as Brody called in the request.

"Oh, yes. We will."

They stepped in the elevator, Julian clenched his hands, then unclenched them. "I can't wait to hear how the reporter heard about her being here."

"We'll find out soon enough. But him getting into her room yesterday, he got his own confirmation." Brody stopped to talk to the officer stationed outside her door.

Julian couldn't wait. He knocked on the door, then stepped inside.

Sophia's eyes were puffier and bloodshot, clearly having been crying. Charlie sat beside her, patting her shoulder. No more than a few years separated the two ladies, but Charlie definitely wore a lioness's protective face.

Her doctor, the one Julian had seen many times, made notations in her chart.

"We had to unplug the phone." Charlie hurled it at him like an accusation.

Sophia looked up at him with such a helpless expression and such pain rimmed in her swollen eyes. It took every ounce of his strength not to forget himself and just pull her into his arms.

"My coach called. He yelled. Screamed. Said I should have called him as soon as I could. Said I'd deliberately tried to sabotage the team just because I couldn't compete." Tears filled her eyes, then spilled over, running down her cheeks.

Even with her beaten face, she cried more beautifully and gracefully than anyone he'd ever seen before. If it didn't nearly rip his heart out through his chest, he'd think it artful the way she cried.

Charlie glared at him. "I hung up on her coach. And the gazillion reporters who won't stop calling. I told the nurses not to put calls through, but they keep calling. They kept upsetting Sophia, so I unplugged the phone entirely."

"Totally understand." He stared at Sophia. "I'm so sorry. I don't know how the information got out."

"My coach is furious, and rightfully so. I knew I should have contacted him."

"Shh. You couldn't. You couldn't talk, and we wouldn't let you." He moved closer and started to stroke her hair, but jammed his hand into his pocket to stop himself.

She just continued to cry. Silently.

It ripped him apart. He didn't know how much longer he could stand to watch her go through this after everything she'd already endured.

"Hey, you were right. He is a weasel." He flashed her a smile he hoped reassured her.

"What?"

"The guy who you said looked like a weasel, who came in yesterday posing as a doctor? We're pretty certain he's the reporter."

"Can't you charge him with impersonating a doctor or something?" Charlie asked, because Sophia never moved her lips.

"Did he actually tell you he was a doctor?"

Charlie looked at Sophia, who shook her head.

"Well, we're bringing him in for questioning anyway." And Julian had quite a bit he planned to say to the man.

"So what now?" Sophia mouthed and Charlie asked.

"Now we figure out where to move you to keep you the safest. It's a fair bet to say this hospital is no longer secure enough. Too many people, too many ways in and out for us to be able to monitor." Julian turned to the doctor. "Is she okay to be moved?"

"Well, we'd like to keep her, of course, but considering the circumstances . . . I'll put a call in to her surgeon and make sure, but I think it will be okay to discharge her to outpatient." Dr. Rhoads headed out of the room, clutching her chart.

"I can't go back there. Not to my mother's home." Sophia's eyes were wide.

"No, of course not. We'd never expect you to." Julian shifted his weight from one foot to the other.

"I'm basically homeless. I'd released my apartment when I made the team, knowing I wouldn't be there for many months."

Julian had never felt more helpless. He'd offer his place in a heartbeat, but knew he couldn't. And he shouldn't—for more than one reason. He looked at Charlie.

"Well, I would say you could stay with me, but my brother's visiting and camping out on my couch."

No, he definitely didn't want Sophia around Scott, who was not only handsome, but a nice guy to boot. Before he could analyze the thought, Brody walked in. "Sorry to have eavesdropped. We'll find you a safe house. One where we can give you twenty-four hour, seven-days-a-week protection. It'll just take us a couple of days to get it set up."

"Nonsense." Alena Borin marched into the room and right to Sophia's bedside. "I am her *Babushka*. Of course, she will stay with me."

His cell rang. "Excuse me," he said, stepping out into the hall as he answered. "Detective Julian Frazier."

"Detective, this is dispatch. Captain Pittman said to notify you of a fire. At the residence of Nina Montgomery. Fire department arrived and put out the fire, but they report a total loss."

And now Sophia's childhood home was gone. She truly was homeless.

13

Sophia didn't know how to react. Right now, her emotions were in such bunches that she couldn't think. All she could hear in her head was Coach Douglas yelling over the phone.

Had she been subconsciously trying to sabotage the team by accepting the police's instructions that she couldn't tell her coach she would be unable to compete with the team? Was she, deep down, so shallow?

Lord, please help me. I don't want to be petty and shallow, but I can't help the way I feel. Right now, I don't even know what to do. Help me.

"You will stay with me, *MIlaya Moyna*. I will nurse you back to health." Alena smiled softly at Sophia. "I will not let anyone harm you."

She'd only just met her grandmother, but Sophia believed Alena.

"I'll get Scott to a hotel. Or, he can stay with Julian. Then you can just stay with me until they find you a safe house." Charlie nodded at Julian as he returned to the room. "Right, Julian?"

"Um. I don't know how to tell you this, Sophia."

"What is it?"

"I just got a report that your mother's house has burned down."

"H-How?"

"I don't know more than that yet. We'll get a report later."

What else, Lord?

"It's decided then. You'll come home with me," Charlie announced.

"No," Sophia mouthed. She couldn't let Charlie dislocate her brother. It was absurd, even if her mother's place had burned down.

"It's fine. Scott can hang out at your place, huh, Julian?" Charlie asked.

"Sure." He nodded, but Sophia could see he wasn't 100 percent sure it was the best idea. Or maybe he was just concerned about the fire. Surely, it meant evidence at the house had been destroyed. Did that hurt the case?

She shook her head at Charlie. "No."

"Come on, Sophia. It'll be fun."

As much as she wanted to say yes, she couldn't. She could not put out these people who she'd only known for days, but already felt such a kinship with. "No. I'll stay with Alena."

Charlie shook her head.

"Yes. It's best."

"We'll have fun."

"Yes, we would. But I need to be with someone who knew my mother. Someone I can grieve with."

Charlie hesitated, then nodded.

"What?" Julian asked.

"She wants to stay with Alena."

"If it's okay," Sophia mouthed and Charlie spoke.

"Of course, my child. We should be together. To mourn my Nina, your *mamochka*. We can share memories."

And there was another reason she wanted to stay with Alena. There was much about her mother she didn't know, and she wanted to know all she could. Sad it was now . . . too late, but it would help her keep her memories of her mother alive in her heart.

"Mrs. Borin, we'll need to come to your house and make sure it's secure. You live in Hot Springs, correct?"

She nodded. "My house is safe. You do not have to come see it."

"Ma'am, actually, we do. It's our job to make sure your grand-daughter is safe." Brody smiled at Alena, who nodded.

The charge nurse from last night entered, holding Sophia's chart to her chest.

Brody took a step toward Alena. "Why don't I go with you to make sure everything's okay? I'm sure the doctors will take their sweet time discharging Sophia. I know you want everything to be just right to make her feel comfortable."

"*Da.*" Alena turned to Sophia. "I will see you soon, *MIlaya Moyna.*" She let Brody lead her out of the room.

"Dr. Rhoads has contacted Dr. Davies and we'll be releasing you soon," the nurse said. "I'll be bringing you the post-operative and discharge instructions in a few minutes. We'll go over the details until you're sure of what you need to do. Okay?"

Sophia nodded. This was all so . . . crazy. Being attacked. Her mother being murdered. Surgery. Learning she'd never be able to compete again. And now this . . . concern the attackers would be back to finish her off and the home she'd been raised in burned down. How did her life get so crazy so fast?

Lord, what did I do to deserve all this?

"In the meantime, I thought you might like to put on these scrubs." The nurse lowered the chart to reveal a neatly folded pair of scrubs sitting on top of the chart. She handed them to Charlie. "I know they'll be a little big, but I figured you'd prefer them over the hospital gown."

"Yes. Thank you." The kindness the nurse had shown her . . . Charlie . . . Julian . . . everybody . . . tears formed in her eyes again.

"You're welcome. I'll be back as soon as I have your discharge papers," she said as she headed from the room.

Charlie lifted the clothes. "How about I help you get into these? I'm sure you're sick of the gown."

Julian's face reddened. "I'm going to have a word with the officer outside." He rushed out the door.

Charlie started laughing as soon as the door closed. "I didn't know he could move so fast when he wasn't chasing a criminal."

Sophia let Charlie help her out of bed. Her legs wobbled a bit as she put her weight on them, but she felt stronger than she had since she'd awakened in the hospital.

"You know you could've stayed with me," Charlie said as she held out the scrub bottoms so Sophia could step in them.

"Yes, but I do need to be with Alena. There's a lot about my mother, apparently, I don't know."

"I understand. I'm still going to come by and check on you just like I do in here."

"I'd hoped you would." Sophia smiled. Despite the reasons for being here, she was truly glad she'd met Charlie Wallace. And Julian.

Especially Julian, but she tried to keep thinking about what Charlie had told her. She was just a victim in the case he was working.

That's all.

After getting dressed, she let Charlie steady her as she began walking laps around the room. What had she gotten herself into? She had no idea where Alena lived. What if it was apartments and hers was upstairs? Sophia would never make it up the stairs.

"Soph?"

She looked at Charlie. "I know you're strong and can kick butt and all, but you need to be careful. I know Julian and Brody will give you a list of a gazillion things they don't want you to do. It'll seem excessive and your instinct will be to just nod and not pay attention. You can't do that."

"I wouldn't."

"You think so, but trust me, their orders will be many and frustrating for someone like you."

"Someone like me how?" What was wrong with her?

"Strong. Independent. Used to doing things for herself."

Sophia gave a little smile. "How do you know me so well?"

Charlie blushed. "I'll be honest, I watched a video of you on the Internet." She shook her head. "You blew me away."

"Not anymore." Sophia glanced at her hands. *Why, God? Why?* She'd never blow anyone away again.

"Don't say that. You're a strong woman. Determined. And yes, you can't compete again, but you could do what your mother did."

"What?" Get herself killed for hiding something? Yeah, it was real smart. The more she thought about it, the madder she got at *Mamochka*. It was incredibly selfish to do something to put her life in jeopardy.

"You could become an instructor. A gymnast coach."

Sophia shook her head. Charlie didn't understand. Coaches weren't disgraced former gymnasts. Coaches were people with the knowledge and ability to teach. There was no place for her in the gymnastic world anymore.

"I'm sorry. I don't mean to upset you."

Sophia swallowed the tears. "No, it's okay. I'm fine."

A knock sounded, followed by Julian's voice, "Okay to come in?"

Sophia looked at Charlie and smiled. "Yeah, come on in."

Julian came in and then shuddered to a stop. "Wow, you're up walking."

"Yeah, I'm supposed to. Get my strength back and all."

"I know. I just hadn't seen you up and about." He smiled, and her heart melted. "You look good on two feet."

"Thanks, but I'm still clumsy." Not graceful like she used to be. People used to describe her as lithe and having contained and controlled power much like a panther.

Not anymore.

"Not so much. Pretty soon, you'll be ready to go out dancing."

Her stare locked onto him. "Is that so?"

Charlie shot her a look that sent Sophia's embarrassment level into the red zone. "I'm just teasing."

"No. It's a date. I'll take you dancing when you're steady on your feet again."

Charlie snorted. "You? Julian Frazier . . . dancing? You don't dance."

Julian turned red. "I do dance."

"Since when?"

"Since none of your business."

"Charlie, leave him alone," Sophia mouthed. "You're embarrassing him."

"Okay," Charlie told her.

"Okay, what?" Julian asked.

"Okay, I'll ask about shoes for her." Charlie winked at Sophia.

Wow, the girl was scary-good on cover-up. Sophia needed to remember that among other things.

Like Julian had promised to take her dancing.

Dancing?

Had he lost his ever-loving mind? He hated dancing. Girls he used to date kidded him about being born with two left feet. Now he'd invited the daughter of a prima ballerina to go dancing?

Was he insane?

Before he could figure out a way to get out of his offer without hurting Sophia's feelings, Dr. Rhoads came back into the room.

The doctor smiled at Sophia and touched her arm, and unexpectedly, a strange sensation came over Julian. The desire, a strong desire, to punch the doctor right in his smiling face.

Where had *that* come from?

The doctor looked up. "Everyone, I'll have to ask you to step outside, please. I need to examine my patient before discharge."

Charlie walked out with Julian. "Hey, I'm sorry about what I said to you yesterday."

He stopped and faced her. "About what?"

"Lecturing you about your interest in Sophia."

"Oh." He'd replayed their conversation over in his head several times as he'd tried to sleep last night. "No, you were right."

"Julian, I had no business saying anything to you."

"No, you're right."

"If you and Sophia are attracted to each other, it's none of my business."

"It's okay—" Wait a minute. Did she mean . . . "What are you saying? Has Sophia said anything about me?"

"Oh, mercy. I am not going to do this. We aren't in high school. If you want to know what the girl thinks about you, you'll have to ask her or figure it out on your own."

"Charlie, come on. One day you're telling me to stay away from her and the next you're hinting she might be interested. You can't yo-yo me around like this."

She groaned. "Now's not the time, either way."

"You're right." He chastised himself for acting like a school-boy. What was next, sending her a note that read: Do you like me? Circle Yes or No. He shuddered.

"I hope she's going to be okay at Alena's," Charlie said.

"Me, too, but Brody won't let her go there if the place isn't secure." Julian checked his watch. "We won't move her until tonight. Less chance of her being seen and us being followed. If we are, then she can't stay there."

"It's not what I meant. I hope she's okay being with Alena. She just met the woman she thought was dead, found out she wanted Sophia aborted, and now is going home with her. I just don't know."

Said like that . . . "Do you have any other suggestions? It looked like it was her choice and you tried to argue with her."

"I know." Charlie hugged her arms and leaned against the hall-way wall. "She's strong and all, but after everything . . . I just worry she's more emotionally fragile than she lets on."

"Really?" His protectiveness threatened to rear its ugly head.

"But, she has her faith, and it's strong, which is good. God will get her through this. I just hate to see her suffer any more."

"I do, too." Julian couldn't shake the feeling in his gut. The feeling . . . there was something about Sophia Montgomery . . .

"On the other hand, when Alena was here last night and she and Sophia were talking about Nina and the quilt, they seemed to get along. Maybe Sophia's right and she does need to spend time with her grandmother to learn more about her mother."

"I guess. I just find it hard to believe Alena would know more about Nina than Sophia. Seemed to me that Nina cut her mother out of her life and was done with her."

"Maybe so, but there's a lot about Nina's past before Sophia that Alena can share with her. Things like she told Sophia last night about Nadia and Dimitri."

"Nadia and Dimitri?" Something seemed familiar about . . .

"Yeah. According to Alena, Nina and Dimitri dated a bit before she met Sophia's dad. Alena claims Nina broke Dimitri's heart. Nadia was her best friend, according to Alena, although Sophia had never heard her mom mention Nadia before. Anyway, Nadia took Nina's place for a time after Nina married Sophia's dad and left the ballet. Also, again, according to Alena, Nadia and Dimitri became an item, until she was killed."

"Killed?" He hadn't heard any of this.

Charlie nodded. "Alena said she was murdered backstage during the *Nutcracker* ballet. She said the costume, the center, focal point on the quilt isn't Nina's, but Nadia's. The Sugar Plum Fairy costume Nadia wore in the *Nutcracker,* which ended up being her final performance."

14

Darkness threatened to swallow her.

Sophia took a deep breath, keeping the wrapped baby doll close in her arms. The wig she wore itched something crazy, but they only had a few more feet until she'd move from the wheelchair to Julian's car.

The disguise had been Charlie's idea, which was both good and bad. Brilliant to hide her identity from the press as a woman who'd just had a baby and Julian was the father taking them home from the hospital. Bad because it made Sophia think about Julian in ways she shouldn't.

She was just a victim in a case he was working.

Charlie was on the other side of the hospital, getting ready to come out of her room with a hoodie over her head and let Brody lead "Ms. Sophia Montgomery" into his squad car. They'd "leaked" it over the hospital that Sophia would be checking out tonight. If the reporter's source was someone in the hospital like Brody claimed after interrogating him, then the press would be waiting to pounce on Charlie as the decoy.

"Almost here, honey," Julian said.

Even though Sophia knew he was just playing the part for anybody who might overhear him, his term of endearment sent heat spreading out from the pit of her stomach.

He pushed the wheelchair to the curb where his car was already parked. He opened the back door, took the doll from Sophia, and bent, pretending to fasten the doll into a non-existent car seat. He straightened and shut the back door quickly. "He's all set, sweetheart. Let me help you." He helped ease her out of the wheelchair, careful to keep her hands covered with her mother's quilt.

"Congratulations. We just had our fourth," a man pushing his own wife, holding a baby, in a wheelchair. "A girl. How about you?"

Sophia's eyes locked onto Julian's. What happened if they asked her a question? They'd get suspicious if she didn't answer.

"A boy. Our first." He leaned closer to the friendly man. "My wife's a little exhausted. Wore slap out. She's almost falling asleep sitting up."

"Oh, honey, you'll get used to it. You'll be amazed at how little sleep you can function on," the other woman called out.

"We're going to stay at her mother's for a bit. Let her help us out with the new baby and all." Julian maneuvered his body between her and the overly chatty couple.

She plopped down into the passenger's seat. He fastened her seatbelt, then planted a quick kiss on the tip of her nose before backing out and shutting the door. Her mouth was totally dry.

"Congratulations to you both," Julian said as he rushed to slip behind the steering wheel. He put the car in gear and eased out of the hospital's front circle.

He glanced in his rearview mirror several times, then seemed to relax. He looked over at her. "You okay?"

She nodded, for once, glad she had an excuse not to speak because her tongue was still tied into knots.

"It shouldn't take more than fifteen minutes to get to Alena's place. Brody checked it out and said it's nice."

She nodded again.

"Brody and Charlie will run by the store and pick up some items she's adamant you must have. They'll keep circling and doubling around until they're sure no one's following them, then they'll meet us at Alena's."

She nodded again, starting to appreciate how a bobble-head character felt.

"Our team is working on securing you a more permanent safe house. It shouldn't take more than a couple of days."

Sophia smiled in the darkness. A more permanent safe house. How long would she need protection? How long could Julian's department afford to give it? What if the attackers weren't even from here? What if they were from another town . . . another state, and were long gone by now? How would she know? Was she destined to just live under police protection for the rest of her life or until someone tried to kill her again?

She glanced at Julian. Being under his protection for the rest of her life wouldn't be the worst thing that could happen.

Stop it! She was just part of the case to him. Nothing more. A witness. A victim.

"The report from the fire department states they believe the fire was set. They're pretty sure it was arson."

Panic welled in the back of her throat. What was she going to do with the rest of her life? She couldn't compete any more. She didn't have any money set aside to go back to college. Her life was over. She'd be a washed up has-been selling sports gear at the local athletic superstore.

"Hey, are you okay?" Julian took his eyes off the road to look at her. "Sounds like you're hyperventilating."

She concentrated on slowing her breathing. In. Out. In.

"Are you in pain? Is the seatbelt hurting you?"

She shook her head. Slow breath in, long breath out. Steady. Rhythmic.

"You're all right?"

Sophia nodded. Drat it! She'd meant to ask Dr. Rhoads about her voice. Could she try it tomorrow?

"Sorry, I don't have a radio or anything in the car. I haven't gotten around to installing one in my baby." He patted the dashboard. "Since I have your undivided attention and you can't tell me to shut up, I'll tell you about Maggie here. Maggie's a 1972 Dodge Charger. She's been through a lot, but I found her and fixed her up. Restored her to her prime condition. Took me three years, but worth every day I spent working on her." Again, he lovingly patted the car.

If he was this affectionate with a car, how did he act with the women he dated?

Ouch. Just the thought of him dating someone made Sophia want to throw up. What did it mean? What did it say about her? Was she just some hopeless romantic sap with an overactive imagination?

Probably.

"My old partner named her. Maggie May. As in Maggie may start, and Maggie may not." He chuckled, a deep, reverberating laugh.

It warmed Sophia's heart more than it should have. She smiled at him.

"Yeah, Eli was quite the comedian."

Eli, not Brody. She cocked her head to the side.

"Oh." He stopped smiling. "You want to know what happened to Eli."

She nodded.

She could hear him swallow in the darkness. "Well, an undercover team had infiltrated a drug cartel. We were in on the bust. Somehow or another, we got separated. The drug group went a little crazy when we stormed them. Started shooting." He shook his head. "When the smoke cleared, Eli was dead on the ground." Julian's voice cracked.

Sophia wanted to hug him. Hold him. Tell him it was okay. But she couldn't do any of those things. Slowly, she twisted in the seat to face him and reached out. She let her fingers slip down the side of his face.

Slowly. Carefully. Deliberately.

His jaw tightened under her touch, and heat shot up her arm as her nails grated against stubble. The car hesitated as he took his foot off the gas pedal. She jerked her hand back to her lap.

"Sophia," he growled, making her heart stutter.

Was he feeling the attraction at all, or was it all in her mind? Blood rushed to her head. She slowly exhaled.

God, I'm in deep here. What do I do? Is what I'm feeling wrong?

He cleared his throat and turned the car into a driveway. "We're here."

Thank goodness they'd arrived, because Julian didn't know if he could resist the urge to pull over to the side of the road and pull Sophia into his arms and kiss her until she lost her senses. When she'd touched his face . . .

Man, he'd never felt so vulnerable, yet so close to someone before. It was nice and strange and scary all at the same time.

He popped both their seatbelt releases then turned in the seat to face her. "Sophia." He could get lost looking into her eyes. The honesty of them. Of her.

The porch lights flicked on.

Julian jumped back. "Your grandmother's on the porch waiting for us." He got out of the car, ran around and opened her door, draped the quilt over his arm, then gently helped her stand. Just touching her elbow made his heart pound.

He had it bad. Real bad. Where was Charlie to lecture him when he needed it?

"Come on inside." Alena held the front door open for them.

Julian led Sophia across the threshold. She walked to the couch in the living room and sat down. He felt ill at ease, not at all like the detective he was.

Alena shut the front door and locked it. Flipped the deadbolt. "I make you nice cup of tea, Sophia. Just like your *mamochka* used to drink it."

Sophia smiled, then tilted her head toward Julian.

"Oh. Would you like a cup, *politseyskiy*?"

He could only assume that meant policeman. "Yes. Thank you."

Alena nodded and left. The sound of water running came from the other room.

Julian smiled at Sophia, feeling more awkward than ever. What was he supposed to say? Tell her just her touch sent him spiraling out of control? And in the back of his mind, he could hear Charlie's words, that Sophia had never been kissed by someone over the age of twenty-one. The thought made him happy, although he knew it shouldn't.

He wanted to be the first *man* to kiss her.

Whoa! Where had that come from?

His cell rang. He snatched it off his belt holder and stood. "Excuse me," he told Sophia as he unlocked the front door and stepped outside. "Detective Frazier."

"Detective, this is Lee in forensics."

Excitement rose in his chest. "Yes?"

"We got the DNA results back from the sample taken from Nina Montgomery's blouse."

"And?" The techs liked drawing stuff out. Must watch too much *CSI* and the like.

"We ran it through CODIS and got a match. DNA belongs to one Boris Taras. His report is being sent to your desk right now."

"Thanks."

"Detective, this isn't all."

"Oh?"

"We pulled the stains on the center part of the quilt. . . all of the samples are blood."

"You're sure?" Sophia had seemed to think it was a soda or something.

"One hundred percent. Tests on them should be complete tomorrow, but initial testing did reveal something I thought you might find interesting."

"What?"

"There are two different types of blood, and neither is Nina Montgomery's type."

"You're positive?"

"Yes, sir. Like I said the test results will be in tomorrow afternoon."

"Thanks, Lee. Keep me posted. I appreciate it."

———

She shouldn't have touched him, but she hadn't been able to stop herself. Now he felt uncomfortable and things were awkward between them. Just when he'd started to treat her like a person and not part of his case, talking about his car and his partner.

Sophia stared at the front door. How could she make it right between them?

"Here is your tea. With sugar and milk, just like Nina used to drink it." Alena set the steaming cup on the table beside the couch. A straw was inside.

Very thoughtful of her to remember. Sophia smiled her thanks.

"I am happy you are here, Sophia. We have missed much time to make up." Alena smiled at her. "You look very much like my Nina when she was little girl."

Sophia smiled and nodded. She'd seen the pictures of her mother as a young mother. They did bear a strong resemblance.

Julian came back inside. He sat on the little settee across from Alena. She handed him a cup. "Your tea. I did not know if you wanted milk or sugar or lemon, so I added in nothing."

"It's fine." He took a sip, grimaced, then set it down. He pointed at the quilt. "Charlie mentioned you learned it's not Nina's costume?"

"No, my Nina was never Sugar Plum Fairy. She was always Clara in the *Nutcracker*. That was Nadia's costume."

"Are you sure?" he asked Alena.

"*Da*. I go to see Nadia perform the night before she killed. It is her costume."

"But you don't remember your mother ever mentioning Nadia's name?" Julian asked Sophia.

She shook her head, wishing Charlie was here.

"I do not know why. They were best friends." Alena took a sip of her tea. "Perhaps after Lance died, my Nina regret not choosing Dimitri and got jealous of Dimitri and Nadia being couple."

Was she kidding? Sophia shook her head. She might not know her mother as well as she thought she did, but the thought of *Mamochka* being jealous over another man? Ludicrous.

"Do not be so sure, Sophia. Your *mamochka* was with Dimitri for a time. He would do anything to make her happy. She broke his heart when she married your father. He only go with Nadia to forget Nina." Alena stood, lifting her empty cup. "Anybody want more tea?"

Sophia and Julian both shook their heads.

As soon as Alena was gone, Julian leaned forward, closer to Sophia. "The stain on the bodice there . . . it's not a soda spill like you thought. It's blood. And not your mother's type. Let me see." He pulled the quilt gently toward him. "Look. See." He pointed to two other areas with red stain droplets. "There are two other areas. All of them are blood. Two different types, and neither of them match your mother's type."

What did that mean? Why was it even important?

. Alena came back into the living room and sat back down in her chair.

Julian looked at Sophia, then at Alena. "Mrs. Borin, do you know a man named Boris Taras?"

Boris who? Where did he get the name from?

"I do."

Julian's eyes lit up like a kid's on his birthday. He inched to sit on the edge of the seat. "How do you know him?"

"He is Dimitri little brother."

15

We need to pull everything we can find on this Dimitri Taras and Nadia Paley." Julian made long strides toward his desk. "Lee said the report on Boris should be on my desk."

Brody matched his pace. "I'll start pulling the reports."

"There has to be a connection to make this whole case come together."

"Captain Pittman was breathing fire over all the media buzz when Charlie and I came in earlier. We've been getting bombarded with calls. Our officer at the Montgomery property has had to call for backups three times already tonight."

"At least the media hasn't yet gotten wind that Nina was killed."

"It's only a matter of time." Brody's fingers went to flying over his keyboard.

Julian found the file Lee had sent over and opened it. He read aloud to Brody. "Boris Taras, thirty-nine, left Russia at the age of three with his father, Igor, and his older brother, Dimitri, and became an American citizen. Sealed juvie records. After turning eighteen, he proceeded with multiple breaking and enterings, thefts, a couple of drug charges, and a half dozen assaults."

"Nice," Brody said. "Do we have an address for this fine, upstanding young man?"

"According to his parole report, last known address is in Little Rock."

"Slide it over here, and I'll call our friends over in the Rock and ask them to pick up Mr. Taras for a little chat with us."

Julian slid the file over to him. While Brody made the call, he opened the case file, updated it, then stared at the blinking cursor.

What did Nina Montgomery have that she didn't want to give to Boris? Something about Dimitri? How did Nadia fit in?

What if Nadia gave Nina whatever it was Boris wanted? She probably could have used Dimitri to gain access to whatever it was.

Which, given his rap sheet, was probably something Boris stole.

What? They'd gone over Nina's house and found nothing worth a lot of money.

"Interesting," Brody interrupted Julian's ponderings.

"What?"

"I got the financials back on Nina Montgomery."

"And?" Julian lifted his key chain and began to spin it around his index finger.

"Every November for the past fifteen years, Nina has received a wire transfer in the amount of fifty thousand dollars."

"What?" Fifty thousand for fifteen years was roughly seven hundred and fifty thousand dollars.

Plenty to kill over.

Brody nodded. "The transfers move from one name to another, through about five different banks. I'll put in a request for our whiz team to do their best to find the point of origin."

"It's insane. Whatever did she spend so much money on?" Julian couldn't comprehend it. Her house, while nice, had been paid for with her husband's life insurance. Same with her studio.

"From what I can tell, looks like the bulk of it was paid directly to Sophia's gymnastic coach and her gym membership."

"So much?" No way!

"About twenty-five grand a year, according to the numbers here." Brody closed the file and shook his head. "I bet Sophia doesn't even have a clue."

"I'm sure she doesn't." Julian recalled how shocked and disappointed Sophia looked when she discovered her mother had lied to her about Alena being alive.

This would devastate her.

"We need to keep this under our hats until we get more information."

"I agree. But looks like we have motive."

"Maybe that's what they were looking for—her bank account information. With her moving it from name to name and bank to bank and around all over, it'd be hard for someone to trace."

"But how would Boris Taras know about the money?"

"Maybe he knew about the annual wire transfers and didn't realize Nina was spending over half of it in a bulk check to cover Sophia's gymnastics lessons. Maybe he thought she had easy access to several hundred thousand dollars, and that's what he was asking for."

Julian swung his key chain around and around. "Could very well be. Definitely a strong motive, but the question still remains—as much as Nina went through to keep the money hidden until she spent it, how did Boris know about the transfers?"

"Maybe once we find the point of origin for the money, we'll have a clue."

"Hope so." Julian stared at the picture of Boris, his stomach twisting as he took in every nuance of the man's face.

Thin face. Slight build. Dirty blond hair. The man who killed Nina Montgomery, most likely. He fit the description Sophia had given of the man who'd been fighting her mother. The one wearing the Russian hat who would've dripped sweat on her blouse.

Julian hung the picture on the board beside their desks. *Who was your accomplice?*

The dead, hateful eyes stared silently back at him.

"Does Boris have any known accomplices?" He scrolled through the case file. "Any known accomplices who match the description of a shaved head, bulky with muscles, stands just under six feet, wears steel-toed boots, and has body odor?"

"Let me check in the system." Brody typed away on his keyboard. After a moment, he hummed. "Well, he has two known accomplices. One is a Chester Milton, and the other is a Donald Obstfeld. Let me see if I can find a description of either."

"Obstfeld. Is he Russian?"

"I have no idea, but his description in no way matches. Donald Obstfeld is five feet five inches, only weighs one hundred and forty-five pounds, wears thick-as-a-bottle-bottom glasses, and works at the Little Rock YMCA." Brody made a few more keystrokes. "Picture is printing."

"I'll get it while you see what you can find on Chester Milton." Julian went to the community printer and pulled off the photo. No way was this the man who'd hurt Sophia. To use her word, this guy looked like a weasel.

Julian hung the photo next to Boris Taras. "How are these two known accomplices?"

"Seems Boris was married to Donald's sister for all of six months before they had the marriage annulled. Donald is linked to several of Boris's drug charges. Prescription drugs stolen and sold on the street."

Definitely not the man who'd crushed Sophia's hands by stepping on them.

Julian stared at Boris's picture while Brody typed. Long moments passed before he stopped typing. "Got it. Chester Milton's picture is printing now, but his description is six foot one, two hundred twenty-five pounds, with short silver hair."

Could be. Julian moved to the printer. The face staring up at him was one of pure evil. Almost as evil as Boris's. He hung the picture next to Boris and Donald's. "I think this is our other guy."

"We can't know for certain. This guy has hair and Sophia said the guy was bald."

"Look how thin it is, Brody. He probably shaves it regularly." It was him. Julian knew it. In his gut.

"We'll get her to look at the picture tomorrow and tell us. Once we know for sure, we can act."

Julian nodded. "Do we have a last known address for Milton?"

"We do. Also in the Rock." Brody lifted his phone. "I'll put in a request for our friends over there to add Mr. Milton to the invitation list for pickup."

"Good."

Brody finished his call.

"How are Taras and Milton connected?" Aside from the attack on Sophia and Nina's murder.

"Chester Milton has been connected to the Taras family ever since they arrived here from Russia. Milton grew up alongside Dimitri and Boris, viewing Igor as a father figure."

"I don't get it. The Taras family has always had money from what I understand, so why did Boris and Milton go the crime route?"

"From what I found out, Dimitri was the Taras golden boy. In ballet, school. People respected him, which Igor liked. He couldn't buy the kind of respectability Dimitri earned by dancing. Being romantically linked with Nina Borin didn't hurt his reputation, either. Remember, she was a star on the rise back in the day. Came straight from Russia to D.C., gaining nothing but momentum as she moved on to New York. Dimitri even partnered with her in a few dances, but it was obvious to the industry and reviewers alike that his talent wasn't even close to hers."

"Could it have been part of the reason for their disenchantment with one another?" Clearly something caused a rift, because she soon was smitten enough with Lance Montgomery to get pregnant and marry him.

"There's nothing on it," Brody answered.

"What about Nadia Paley?"

"It's loading now."

Julian spun his key chain. Faster and faster.

"Nadia Paley. Member of the New York City Ballet. Aged twenty-two at her time of death. She was found dead in her dressing room, backstage after her performance in the *Nutcracker* sixteen years ago."

Twenty-two years old . . . a crime to die so young. "Alena said she'd been murdered."

"Yes. According to the coroner, cause of death was blunt force trauma to the back of the head. It was labeled a homicide."

"Anyone convicted on the case?"

Brody scrolled through pages on his computer. "No. Nobody was ever charged."

"Really?" Julian set down his keychain and stared at his partner. "Who were their prime suspects?"

"These records don't show any prime suspects. A couple of fellow dancers were investigated, but nothing came of the inquiries."

"That's New York for you."

Brody shook his head. "She didn't die in New York."

"She didn't? Where'd she die?" Julian asked.

"In Arkansas. Little Rock."

"That's insane." Julian shook his head.

"It's a tragedy is what it is. Beautiful young ballerina murdered, and they can't even build a case to charge someone? It's a tragedy."

"But yet you believe in God?" Julian held up his hands, instantly regretting his words. "Sorry, man. None of my business."

"It's okay. Tragedies happen. Murders happen. Crime happens. But in it all, I know it's not of God's doing. It's men's doing."

"But isn't God all powerful and all that?"

Brody laughed. "Yeah, he's all powerful and *all that*, but He also gave us free will. Meaning we could choose to follow Him and do what's right, or we can just do whatever we want. He's not a dictator god, Julian, but a loving one. Just like Nina loved Sophia and Alena loved Nina. Both differently, but still love. Alena tried to force her wishes on Nina and you see how well it turned out. God doesn't want us to go and do our own thing, but He'll allow us to make our own mistakes."

"I guess."

"Think about it this way. Every day, we see kids choosing the life of crime even though their parents are good, upstanding people. Were there as hands-on parents. Did everything they could to provide for the kids. Family dinners together, family vacations and all the usual, but the kids still turn out to be rapists or thieves or murderers, right?"

"Yeah. Nobody said it was the parents' fault the kids went bad."

"Exactly." Brody smiled.

Huh? "I'm not following you."

"Well, God's our heavenly Father. Mine, yours . . . everybody's. But when we choose to go bad and do bad things, it's on us, not our Father." Brody grinned. "Get it?"

"Yeah. I follow you. Just not sure I buy it."

"Hey, I'm not selling it. Just telling you how it is."

Brody's computer beeped.

He clicked and then scrolled. "Well, isn't this interesting."

"What?"

"Just got my query on Dimitri Taras back."

Julian reached for his key chain. "And?"

"You already know a lot of it. Coming to Russia. Dancing. Linked romantically to Nina Montgomery, then Nadia Paley."

"Yeah, yeah, yeah."

"Here's the interesting bits. Seems Mr. Taras had been looking for Nina. Privately."

This was interesting. "When?" Julian asked.

"Starting a decade ago."

"Really? Any idea what prompted it?"

"I don't know. But he's kept the file open. All extremely confidential." Brody leaned back in his chair.

"Where's Dimitri now?"

"Still has his primary residence in New York. He travels a lot. To Russia. Has financial ties to many ballet companies and academies. Funds a lot of troupes. He has season tickets to several dance companies."

"Any indication he found Nina?"

Brody shook his head. "The file's still open and as far as I can tell, he's never been given a lead to link her to being in Arkansas."

Julian stared at the pictures on the board.

"What're you thinking?" Brody asked.

"I'm thinking it can't be a coincidence. Dimitri has a past tie to Nina. His brother and accomplice attack Sophia and Nina, asking her where it is before killing her. The Taras family has money. Nina was receiving a large amount of money every year anonymously, and she worked hard to make it untraceable." Julian shook his head. "What are we missing here?"

Brody stood up. "I don't know, partner, but it's late and I'm tired. Let's call it a night and see what we come up with tomorrow morning."

"Deal." Julian shut down his computer. "I'll take these photos by Alena's in the morning and see if Sophia can identify Boris and Milton."

He'd hate to traumatize her, but if she identified them, then they could have the Little Rock police arrest them. Once they had them in custody, they could get answers.

And maybe Sophia could get a little peace.

16

No! Stay away from my daughter. She knows nothing."

Mamochka!

Sophia's head exploded in bursts of pain and flashes of light. She couldn't see. Everything was dim.

"Gde kostyum?" *his voice loud, echoing.*

"*I don't know what you're talking about.*"

"*Come on, Nina. You do. Look, your* doch *is unconscious. You can protect her by telling us where you have hidden it.*"

Mamochka *screamed, but Sophia couldn't open her eyes. She could barely breathe her chest hurt so much. Lord, please help me. Make them stop. Save us!*

"*You can make it end. Tell us where it is and we will leave.*"

"*No.*"

"*Nina, Nina, Nina. Do you think he wanted to hurt you? Do you think he wanted it to come to this? No. You know he did not. But this is your fault. You should have never started the* shantazhirovali. *You knew he could be dangerous, no?*"

"*Just go away,*" Mamochka *cried.*

"*You know we can't, Nina. We must get what we came for, or he will be angry. Just tell us where it is.*"

"No."

"Then your doch, your gold medal Sophia will pay."

Her face slapped . . . hard, jolting her eyes open.

His hand, balled into a fist, coming down to her chest.

Sophia bolted upright, her breathing in small pants and gasps. She swallowed as she kicked the bedcovers off.

It took her a moment to remember where she was—Alena's house.

She stared at the bedside clock. Five ten. The sun hadn't even begun to creep its way up. She leaned over and got a sip of water. Her breathing became less erratic.

Had she experienced a memory pulled from her subconscious? She didn't remember it happening, but maybe it was a suppressed memory coming up. If it was, what did it mean?

Carefully, Sophia climbed out of bed and headed to the restroom across the hall. As she put on the protective gloves, she studied herself in the mirror. Her face wasn't nearly as swollen and the bruising looked much better.

Sophia leaned in closer to the mirror. But . . . she looked . . . different. Older, somehow.

She stood back. Haunting is what it was. It was the haunting look in her eyes. The tragedy she'd lived through . . . was living through. And the truly scary part was she recognized the look, because she'd seen it in her mother's eyes on those times she caught her mother in unguarded moments.

What had haunted her mother? Losing her husband, yes, but there was more to it, Sophia just knew it. There were too many times Sophia would catch her mother just staring off into space, or at the quilt hanging on the wall, and the same look would creep into her eyes as was reflected in Sophia's right now.

"Sophia, are you okay?" Alena called out from the hall.

She finished up and stepped out into the hallway.

Alena, fully dressed, stood outside the bathroom door. "Are you ready for me to make you some breakfast? The coffee is already hot."

She hadn't planned on being up so early, but why not? She smiled and nodded, following Alena into the kitchen.

"It is so nice to have you here, Sophia. Almost like having Nina home again." She poured a cup of coffee and stuck a straw in it.

Sophia's pulse stalled. She wasn't a replacement for her mother. It was kinda creepy the way Alena kept lumping them together in her mind.

"I will make you good *zavtrak*. Do you like boiled eggs and *kasha*?"

Boiled eggs and porridge? Well, why not? Sophia nodded.

"Good. I make it for you." She pulled out one of the chairs at the kitchen table. "Sit. Sit. I will make you good food, so you can get strong and well, yes?"

Sophia slipped into the chair. If only she could talk, she could ask Alena what *gde kostyum* and *shantazhirovali* meant. They were part of her dream she remembered vividly, but were spoken in the Russian she didn't understand. Her mother had been reluctant for her to learn any Russian.

Looking at Alena, Sophia had to wonder if she was the reason why. Had *Mamochka* been so hurt by her mother that she would even turn away from her heritage?

Alena sat the coffee with the straw on the table in front of her. "Did your mother cook for you? She was good in kitchen." She turned and put eggs on to boil.

Sophia smiled and nodded. Her mother had indeed been an excellent cook. She'd loved to make big meals for them to share together. Once Sophia started training, *Mamochka* had changed the way she cooked in order to accommodate Sophia's training diet.

"She and Nadia were always cooking something. Making a big mess, too, but the food was good. Very, very good."

Who was Nadia to be such an important part of her mother's young adult life, but she never mentioned her to Sophia? It almost felt like she'd kept her past a secret from Sophia on purpose. But why?

"Nadia was not as good as cook, just like she not as good as dancer as Nina. But that was okay. Nadia and Nina, they were like sisters. Until your father came along." Alena began making the porridge from various different grains.

Sophia sipped her coffee through the straw, hanging on Alena's every word.

"At first, I think it because Nadia jealous of Nina, but then I realize she wants Nina to be with your father, because she wants Dimitri. She always wanted whatever Nina had. She was jealous. Not in a bad way, just envious of Nina dancing and life."

Healthy competition, perhaps?

"When Nina tell us she is pregnant, I made Nadia swear never to tell anyone. If Nina would do as I said, no one but Nadia would have known." Alena shook her head and adjusted the fire under the porridge. "I thought Nina and Nadia would stay friends even after she married Lance, but they did not. Maybe because Nadia was with Dimitri. Maybe your *mamochka* was a little jealous. A flip between them maybe."

Sophia shook her head. She couldn't imagine her mother jealous over a man. Especially not someone she'd frowned over every time she'd mentioned his name.

Or had she been frowning because he was with another woman? Had it been too painful for her to think of them together, so she couldn't stay friends with her best friend?

No, it couldn't be.

"Ah, but it is in the past, yes? It is time for us to be family now. For me to get to know you."

Sophia took another sip of the coffee. It was as strong as her mother used to make it. Family tradition, perhaps?

Alena pulled bowls from the overhead cabinets and poured the porridge into them, then set them on the table. "The eggs will be ready in a few minutes. Go ahead and start eating your *kasha*."

Sophia bowed her head. *Lord, please bless this food You have provided. Use it for the nourishment of our bodies and our bodies to Your service. In Jesus' name, I pray and give thanks, Amen.* She lifted her head to catch Alena's stare.

"You were praying?"

Sophia nodded.

"That came from your father. Your *mamochka* . . . she did not pray like this."

Yes, she did. They prayed together. When Sophia was a child, her mother would kneel alongside her at bedtime and pray the "Now I Lay Me Down to Sleep" prayer with Sophia.

"Your father made her follow his beliefs. Nina did not do that on her own."

Well, Sophia was sure glad her father had led *Mamochka* to Jesus. At least, Sophia could rest assured she'd see both her parents again.

Sophia decided she couldn't argue the issue with Alena even if she wanted to, so she gently set the spoon in her hand, laying it to where she could use her fingertips to manipulate the silverware. She took a bite of the porridge. A bit bland in taste, but it was good. Dr. Rhoads said she could move up to soft foods, and she was thankful to have something more than broth, yogurt or gelatin.

"It is good?"

Sophia nodded her thanks.

Alena smiled wide and for a moment, Sophia could see a glimpse of her mother's face in the lines around Alena's eyes. "I will help you get cleaned up after we eat. If you want me to help you. I can wash your hair for you."

Oh, yes, it sounded heavenly. Sophia smiled and nodded.

"Then we will get you fixed up to feel better, yes?"

The phone rang, and Sophia jumped.

"It is okay, *MIlaya Moyna*. It is just the phone." She stood and grabbed the phone from the living room table before it could ring again. "Hello."

A pause, then, "Hello?" Another pause, then she hung up the phone and returned to the kitchen.

"Nobody said anything. Must be wrong number." Alena moved to take the eggs off the stove.

Wrong number, or had she been found again? This time by the men who had murdered her mother?

He hated himself for having to do this, but he had no choice. Not if he wanted to solve this case.

Julian let out a sigh and pushed the doorbell.

The curtain in the window next to the door fluttered, then the locks disengaged and Alena opened the door.

"Good morning, Mrs. Borin."

"Detective." She moved aside and waved him in, then locked the door behind him. At least she was consistently careful. Julian could appreciate that.

He stood hesitantly in the living room, unsure what to do with himself, which was a new feeling for him. "Mrs. Borin, could you please get Sophia?"

"She cleaning up. She will be here in a minute. She knows you are here." She waved to the couch. "Please. Sit."

He didn't want to sit, but he couldn't be rude, either, so he sat.

"Do you want a cup of coffee?" Alena asked.

"Yes. Thank you."

Alena rushed to the kitchen, as if she couldn't wait to escape his presence. Well, it was awkward.

He set the folder with the pictures on the table and let out a long breath. This was most assuredly going to be upsetting to Sophia, but it had to be done. He just didn't know if he could stand seeing her upset and not comforting her, but his job prevented him from doing that.

Sophia walked into the room and stole his breath away.

Her long, curly hair was pulled back into one of those fancy braids. She wore a tee shirt and a pair of shorts that really showed off her legs. She looked like a Fourth of July celebration.

He managed to climb to his feet. "G-Good morning."

She smiled, pink dotting her cheeks as she sat across from him. She was truly a vision.

And he had to ruin her day.

Julian let out a slow breath and tapped the folder. "I have a couple of photos I need to show you."

She sat up straighter.

"It's pictures of some suspects we have. I need you to let me know if you can positively identify the men who attacked you and your mother."

All the beautiful color drained from her face.

She nodded.

Alena came into the room. Sophia looked up and motioned for her to come sit beside her. Alena did, shooting Julian with inquiring stares.

"We have some suspects, and I need Sophia to look at the pictures to identify if they are the men who attacked her and Nina."

Alena nodded, then put her arms around Sophia's shoulders. "You can do this, *MIlaya Moyna*. Our family women are strong. Very strong."

Julian was glad Alena was here for Sophia. She could provide strength and comfort when he couldn't.

He opened the folder and held up the first picture. The picture of Donald Obstfeld. "Do you recognize this man, Sophia?"

She studied the picture for a long moment, then slowly shook her head.

He put Obstfeld's picture back in the file, then lifted the next photo. Chester Milton. He didn't even have it all the way in front of her before Sophia's eyes widened, her face went whiter than white, and she nodded.

"Is this one of the men who attacked you and your mother, Sophia?"

She nodded, and tears eased down her face.

Alena hugged her closer and whispered to her in Russian.

Julian put the picture away, then reached for the last one. He held it up for Sophia. "Do you recognize this man, Sophia?"

She nodded, more tears escaping.

Alena looked at the picture, and gasped. "I know this man."

"You do?" Julian asked.

"*Da*. It is Boris Taris, brother of Dimitri."

"Yes, it's who he is. Have you seen this Boris in town, Mrs. Borin? Ever?"

Alena shook her head. "I have not seen Boris since the last time I saw Dimitri."

"When and where?"

"In New York, right after Nina moved away with Lance. I went to see Nadia dance. She danced with Dimitri. I told them both after the ballet they were beautiful dancers and I hoped Nina would return to the stage soon. Nadia laughed. Boris was there with his brother."

"And you've not seen them in Arkansas?"

"No. I did know about Nadia dancing in the *Nutcracker* in the state many years ago, but I did not see Dimitri or Boris."

Julian slipped the photograph back into the folder.

"Boris . . . he is one of the men who attacked my Nina and Sophia?"

Sophia nodded. She mouthed something.

Alena shook her head. "I do not understand this lip talking."

Sophia looked at Julian. Even though he wasn't a lip reader, he easily made out what she mouthed: "He killed my mother."

Julian nodded. "Thank you. I'm sorry to have put you through all this." He lifted his folder and stood. "With your positive identification, along with DNA test results, we're having both men picked up and arrested. I'll let you know as soon as we have them in custody."

Alena stood as well, moving to unlock and open the front door for him. "Thank you, Detective. You see Boris and the man pay for killing my Nina."

"Yes, ma'am. That's what I aim to do."

He'd do whatever it took to see the man who did this to Sophia paid, and paid dearly.

17

I can't get over how much better you look," Charlie said. "Must be getting out of the hospital. Those places always make you sicker, I say."

Sophia smiled. "I feel better. Alena washed my hair and braided it. It made me feel almost like a woman again. And taking a long, hot shower with real body wash that didn't rip my skin off was wonderful."

"You reapplied your bandages after your shower just like the nurse showed you, right? And you took your medicine?"

Sophia nodded and held out her hands for Charlie to inspect them.

"Sorry. Just don't want you to get any infections." Charlie leaned back on the couch. "So, how are you doing? Alena told me about Julian's visit this morning."

"It was hard seeing their faces, but I'm glad to know Julian was able to identify them so they can be arrested. Julian said he'd call when they were in custody."

"I've been praying for you."

Sophia smiled. "Thank you. I know it's God who's holding me up through all this. I'd never make it through without Him."

"Amen. But are you okay? I think maybe you should consider speaking to a therapist about the attack."

Sophia shrugged. "I might. Right now, I think I'm doing as well as can be expected. It's hard to look into the face of the man who killed your mother and also killed your ability to keep your career, even if it was only in a picture."

"No, it can be traumatic. It's why I mentioned talking to someone. I know several good people I can recommend. Going through this and then having to relive it over and over to help on the case and then during trial . . . well, it can bring on a wide range of emotions. Nightmares even."

Sophia perked up. "Speaking of nightmares, I need you to write something down for me to ask Alena what it means."

"Okay. Where's something to write with and write on?"

"In the kitchen. Front of the refrigerator."

Charlie returned with a pen and paper. "Okay. Ready."

"*Gde kostyum.*"

"Uh, I'm assuming it's Russian?"

Sophia nodded. "I think it would be spelled g-d- and either e or a. Then c- or k-o-s-t . . . and u-m. I think. And another word: *shantazhirovali*. I think it's spelled s-h-a-n-t-a-z- . . . I think h-i-r-o- . . . and maybe v-a-l- and either i or e. I think"

"Let me see if I can do a search right quick." Charlie pulled out her smartphone and did a search. "Well, it's not the right combination. Let me try another."

The front door opened and Alena stepped inside. "I am home." Her arms full of bags, she kicked the door closed.

Charlie set down her cell phone and jumped up to grab a bag. "Here, let me help."

"Thank you, Charlie." Alena led the way into the kitchen where they set the bags on the counter. "What are you girls doing? You remind me of Nina and Nadia. Always together doing something."

Charlie smiled. "I'm trying to look up how to spell a couple of words in Russian."

"In Russian?" Alena laughed. "I am Russian. I can help you. What are words?"

"Come see." She went into the living room and handed the paper to Alena. "Do you know what it means?"

"*Gde kostyum?*"

Sophia nodded.

"It is asking *where is the costume*?"

"And the other?" Charlie asked.

"Should be *shantazhirovali*?" Alena asked, frowning.

Sophia nodded.

"Means *blackmail*."

Sophia's heart skipped a beat, then went into overdrive. She looked at Charlie. "You need to call Julian to come over here. I need to tell him about my dream."

Charlie tilted her head. "Uh, you want to tell Julian your dream?"

"I thought it was a dream, but it wasn't a dream, I think it was a memory of some sort but I didn't think—"

"Whoa, slow down a minute. Your lips are moving too fast and I can't keep up."

"It wasn't a dream. I was remembering something from the attack. I need to tell Julian."

"Oh. Okay." Charlie dialed Julian.

"This is Detective Julian Frazier. Leave a message." The beep sounded.

"Julian, it's Charlie. I'm with Sophia. When you get a chance, we need you to come by. Sophia remembers something else about the attack she needs to tell you. Give me a call when you get this. Bye." She set the phone on the coffee table. "I guess he'll call as soon as he can."

Sophia closed her eyes and prayed it was soon.

"They've put out a BOLO on both Taras and Milton," Brody told Captain Pittman.

"A be on the lookout for is good, but it also means they aren't in custody," the Captain replied.

"Little Rock PD checked both of their last known addresses. They weren't found at either residence, but neither looked as if they'd been vacated, so we don't have reason to believe they've fled," Julian added.

"The police will be going back to check their residences and known hangouts periodically today. We also have a watch for activity placed upon their credit cards and accounts," Brody said.

Captain Pittman nodded. "I don't have to tell you two how far sideways the press has crawled up my back. The mayor's calling every hour, wanting updates. I'm sure you can understand how I need for you two to be on top of this."

"Yes, sir," they said in unison.

"Okay. Keep me updated," the captain said to dismiss them.

They rounded the corner back to their desks just in time to hear Julian's intercom start ringing. He sprinted to reach it. "Detective Julian Frazier."

"Detective, it's Lee in forensics."

"Whatcha got?"

"Remember we pulled two different types of blood from the quilt sample?"

"Yes."

"Well, we got the DNA back on them today."

Julian sat on the edge of his desk and reached for his key chain. "I'm listening."

"One of the samples, we got a hit on."

"The DNA was in the system?"

"No. We got a hit on familial DNA."

"Uh, I'm not real sure what you mean, exactly, Lee. Let me put you on speakerphone so you can explain it to me and Brody at the same time." He pressed the speaker button and replaced the handset. "Okay, go ahead."

"Basically, familial searching is an additional search of the DNA database conducted after a routine search has been completed and no profile matches are identified. Familial searching is new and is a deliberate search of a DNA database conducted to potentially identify close biological relatives to the unknown forensic profile obtained from crime scene evidence. First-order relatives, like siblings or parental relationships, will have more genetic data in common than unrelated individuals."

Julian looked at Brody, who shrugged. "I'm still not getting it, Lee."

"Okay, when I ran one of the DNA samples I got off the quilt through the system, it didn't come back with a match. It did come back with enough genetic data match to let me know it's a first-order relative to a sample already in the system."

"Who was the match to?" Brody asked.

"Are you ready for this?"

Julian spun his key ring. "Tell me."

"Boris Taras."

"So this means the DNA on the quilt . . ."

"Has to belong to a first relative to Boris. A male relative."

Julian dropped his key ring on the desk. "Thanks, Lee." His mind was ready to explode. Boris only had two first relatives: Igor and Dimitri, and according to records, Igor was dead. That only left Dimitri.

"What about the other sample on the quilt?" Brody asked.

"No hits."

"Thanks, Lee," Brody said.

"I'll have the report sent right over to you guys."

Julian faced his partner. "We need to find out where Dimitri Taras is right now."

Brody's fingers flew over his keyboard. "I'm on it."

This was it. Julian could feel it. They knew who the perps were and had solid forensic evidence to put away both Boris and Milton.

Now . . . how to tie Dimitri into it. It had to be his DNA on the quilt, but why? And whose was the other? It wasn't Nina's.

He lifted his key chain and spun it around his finger. His cell phone beeped, indicating a voice message. Julian played the message and heard Charlie's voice. After erasing the message, he called Charlie's number.

"Hello." She answered on the first ring.

"Hey, Charlie. What's up?"

"Listen, Julian, Sophia had a dream, but it was actually a memory about the attack she needs to tell you about."

"We're in the middle of working the case, Charlie. Can't you just tell me over the phone?"

"Sure. Hang on." There was silence, then she was back. "Okay. She remembers one of the men, she doesn't know which one because she couldn't see, only could hear, and she didn't realize what the words meant until today when I could spell them for Alena to translate."

"Okay."

"They asked Nina, 'where is the costume?' and then mentioned she should have never started the game of blackmail. Sophia says she has no idea what it means, but says she thinks it's important."

Important? It was possible it'd just linked Dimitri Taras to the crime. "It's exactly what I needed to know. Let me work out some angles here, then I'll come there."

"Okay. We'll see you later then."

"Charlie?"

"Yeah?"

"Keep the quilt of Nina's safe, will ya? I think it ties this whole case together."

"Okay."

Julian lifted the intercom and dialed the extension.

"Forensics, this is Lee."

"Just the man I needed to talk to. This is Detective Frazier."

"What can I do for you, Detective?"

"You know the other blood stain you got the DNA from—the one with no matches found in the system?"

"Yes, sir."

"Contact the Little Rock coroner's office. See if they kept a sample on an open homicide from sixteen years ago. Victim's name was Nadia Paley."

"I'm on it."

"Thanks." Julian hung up the phone and told Brody about what Sophia had remembered. "We need the case file on Nadia Paley's murder."

"Let me call Little Rock again and see if they can e-mail us a copy." Brody made the call.

Julian pulled the picture of the quilt out of the stack of case photographs. He stuck it to the center of their board. It was the center of this whole case.

"Got it. Let me open the file." Brody typed. "Okay. What are you looking for?"

"Give me the details of her murder."

"Sixteen years ago, the New York City Ballet company took their production of the *Nutcracker* on tour. Nadia was cast in the role of a Sugar Plum Fairy. I'm printing a picture of the coverage of Nadia in the press to promote the play."

Brody continued. "According to the records, the performance in Little Rock was held on November twenty-first."

November. Interesting. Julian nodded at his partner, the familiar feeling tightening in his gut. The feeling he always got when they were about to blow a case wide open and solve it.

"The performance went as usual, according to reviews, but two hours after the performance, when the stage manager was clearing all the dressing rooms, he found Nadia's body. You already know the coroner's report on cause of death."

Julian nodded, picking his key ring back up and spinning it.

"Fill me in on your theory, partner."

"Let me grab Nadia's photo." He rushed to the printer, smiling as he snatched the printout, and returned to their board. He pinned the picture next to the photograph of the quilt. It was just what he expected. "I think sixteen years ago is when this all started. With Nadia Paley's murder." He pointed to the picture of Nadia, in her costume, then pointed to the center point of the quilt.

"It's the same outfit," Brody said.

Julian spun his key ring. "Yep. The one she was murdered in. I think somehow, some way, Nina Montgomery found out Dimitri killed her friend, Nadia. Even more, she somehow got Nadia's costume with both Dimitri's and Nadia's blood on it, and everybody knew she wore it at the performance in Little Rock."

"Hold on a minute." Brody typed on his computer. "I'm requesting the whereabouts of Dimitri on the night Nadia was murdered." He made a few more keystrokes, then leaned back in his chair. "Okay. Done. Continue."

"So Nina has the costume with both Nadia and Dimitri's blood on it, and she knows Dimitri murdered Nadia."

"Why doesn't she come to the police?" Brody asked. "Nadia was her friend, according to Alena. Why doesn't she come forward?"

Julian sat on the edge of the desk, staring at the board. "Maybe she was scared of Dimitri? For some reason, she didn't tell the police."

ROBIN CAROLL

"Okay. I can buy the whole she-was-scared thing. Sounds like his family was pretty powerful."

"A year passes, and Dimitri doesn't come for her. Maybe, for some reason, she realizes he doesn't know what she knows, and what she has. Now Sophia's talent in gymnastics is coming out, and Nina learns how expensive it'll be for her daughter's training. She doesn't know how she'll afford it but knows she needs it."

"And that's when she decides to play the blackmail card."

Julian nodded at his partner. "Right. Somehow, she contacts Dimitri with the information of what she has and what she knows. She demands payment. Maybe she tells him up front it'll be an annual payment, maybe not. She wasn't greedy, just got enough to live on and pay for Sophia's training."

Brody picked up the theorizing from there. "She sets up an elaborate wiring schedule to keep Dimitri from knowing who is exactly blackmailing him, but the money must come every November."

"Near the anniversary of Nadia's death, to remind him what he did?"

Brody shrugged. "Sounds good."

Julian pinned up the newspaper photograph of Sophia taken at Nina's. "Now, remember Dimitri had been conducting a silent search for Nina for years. When this article hits, with Nina's maiden name included, his investigation tips him off."

Brody nodded. "He sees this photo and despite the graininess, he recognizes Nadia's costume."

"And realizes it's Nina, the woman he'd once loved, who has been blackmailing him all these years." Julian's key ring spun faster and faster. "He's furious, maybe even beyond furious, but also knows he can end the blackmail. End the whole thing."

"So he calls his brother, Boris, and childhood friend, Chester Milton, and tells them to handle his little problem for him."

Julian dropped his key chain onto the desk. "Wait a minute . . ." He flipped through the case files. Page after page. Scanning.

180

Reading. Looking for— "Got it." He pulls out Roger Parrish's statement and pinned it to the board.

"Well? I'm waiting." Brody grinned.

"Nina had to figure out the crazy wiring schedule, and she certainly hadn't a clue how to do it. She needed help. Who better to give such advice than her neighbor who was retired from the financial business?"

"I like it."

"Wait. It gets better." Julian grinned and grabbed his key chain. "Roger and Linda Parrish plan to go see their daughter, and goodness knows they tell everyone. But what's important is Roger had to tell the place where he volunteers, teaching classes to rehabilitated criminals. At the Little Rock YMCA. The same place Donald Obstfeld works."

Brody nodded. "The Donald Obstfeld who is a known associate of Boris Taras." He typed on his computer. "Just in. According to records, at the time of Nadia Paley's murder, Dimitri Taras was supposedly at home in New York City."

"Can we check flights and see if there's proof to the contrary?"

"Won't do any good. Dimitri has his own plane. He lets various ballet bigwigs and such use it. And before you ask," Brody shot Julian a stare across the desks, "the plane was in Little Rock that night and documentation showed several people were on the flight to attend the performance, but Dimitri isn't listed as one of them."

"Easy enough to fudge your own plane's passenger list. We know it can be done."

Brody nodded.

Julian's key ring spun like a top. "So the plan was set into motion. Break into Nina's home, get the costume with the evidence, and kill Nina and Sophia."

"Do you think they realized Sophia would be there?"

Julian nodded, dropping the key chain back to his desk. "I think they planned it well enough so they knew exactly who would be there, and they planned exactly what they'd do to them."

"But they didn't get the costume with the evidence."

"And they didn't kill Sophia." And if Julian had anything to say about it, they wouldn't, but they'd pay for hurting her.

They'd pay dearly.

The phone on Brody's desk rang. "Detective Alexander." A pause.

"Yes." Another pause.

"Where?"

Julian stared at his partner.

"Okay. Thank you." Brody hung up the phone. "There's a hit on Boris Taras's credit card. At a gas station about twenty miles east of Little Rock."

"Think they're heading this way?"

"Don't know. They've dispatched the information to the sheriff's department in the county, and they will call us as soon as they find them."

Julian stared at the picture of Boris on the board.

What are you doing, Boris? What are you up to?

18

"I don't know any more than what he said on the phone," Charlie said.

Frustration squeezed Sophia's heart. She wanted to see Julian, hear what he thought of her memories.

"He did, however, tell me to make sure your quilt stayed safe."

The quilt.

Sophia went to her room, got the quilt, and spread it out over the living room table. She tried to remember what her mother had said about the center costume.

"It is very valuable, Sophia. We must always take care of the things important to us. You never know the true value of something until later. Much later."

Was it possible this costume of Nadia's was what *Mamochka* had been talking about?

"What are you thinking, Sophia?" Alena asked.

"Well, why did my mother keep this costume of her best friend's? Her best friend who was murdered?" Sophia mouthed, running her fingers over the delicate material. "It's a little morbid to put it on a quilt we used as a tapestry as far back as I can remember."

"Is not morbid, *MIlaya Moyna*. Is honoring Nadia. Remembering her."

Sophia shook her head. "No. If it was to honor or remember Nadia, *Mamochka* would have told me about her, like she told me stories about my father."

"Then why?" Alena asked.

"Remembering what I recalled early this morning about the attack, I think she used this costume to blackmail someone in some way."

"For what?" Charlie asked. "I'm sorry, but it wasn't like your mother lived in the lap of luxury. She worked at her studio and paid her bills. I don't see any type of extravagant luxuries. Do you have a big savings account or something?"

Sophia snorted. "I don't even have a college fund. Gymnastics was always my future."

"See. So what would she be blackmailing anybody for?"

"Gymnastics," Alena said.

"What?"

"The training. Coaching. Instructing. All is expensive." Alena wore a pained expression. "I know how expensive it can be. We *mamochkas* want the best for our daughters, so we do what we have to in order to provide for lessons and training."

Sophia stared silently at the costume. Had *Mamochka* blackmailed someone to pay for all of Sophia's gymnastics training? Was this the reason they'd been attacked? And why she was killed?

She blinked, but her vision was still blurred by the tears who ignored her demands they stay at bay.

"Sophia. Are you okay?" Charlie asked.

"It makes sense now. Why she got so upset when the picture in the paper came out. You could see the quilt, the costume. Not clearly, but you could tell it was a ballet costume. If you were familiar enough with the ballet world, you could probably tell what

184

ballet it was from." Sophia gestured toward Alena. "She knew right away it was the costume of a Sugar Plum Fairy in the *Nutcracker*."

"Costumes vary a little bit, but famous ballets do keep the basic design," Alena said.

"My mother must have known whoever she was blackmailing could see the picture and recognize the costume. It's why she was so angry. It's why she took the quilt and hid it in her room."

"This is why my Nina was murdered?" Alena reached for the quilt.

Sophia snatched it up, clutching it to her chest. "No. It's evidence. Julian said to keep it safe. I'm going to go put it up." She went to her room and looked around. Where could she put it?

She remembered her mother's hiding spots. With a sad smile, she opened the closet and looked for a sweater or coat.

A knock sounded on the front door.

Sophia hurried and hung the quilt under an old winter coat, one much too heavy for Arkansas. She carefully closed her bedroom door and moved toward the living room but froze when she heard the voice she'd never forget . . .

"Hello, Alena. It has been a long time."

Her heart lodged in the back of her throat. He was one of the men who attacked her and *Mamochka*!

She turned to run, but the other man, the man who'd crushed her hand, grabbed her. "Well, hello again, Sophia. Why don't you join our little party?" He flung her onto the couch beside Charlie.

Her stomach turned. She was going to be sick.

Charlie put her arm around Sophia's shoulders. "It'll be okay."

"Aww, isn't this sweet?" Boris pointed the gun at Alena. "Where is the costume, old woman?"

"I do not know what you mean."

Without warning, he reached out and slapped Alena across the face. Hard. She fell to the floor.

Sophia trembled. *Dear Lord, help us!*

"Now, let's try again." Boris turned to Charlie. "You. Translator. Tell me where is the costume and we will make this no painful for you."

Charlie sat up straight and stuck out her chin. "What costume?"

"Wrong answer." He slapped her, and she fell across the couch.

Boris pointed the gun at Sophia. "You. Sophia. Miss gold medal. You know what I'm talking about, don't you?"

God, help me!

He squatted down to her eye level. "You don't want us to hurt you again, do you? Not like before. Just show me where the costume is."

She leaned over and threw up all over the coffee table and floor.

Boris jumped backward. "*Otvratitel'no!*"

Charlie handed her a tissue. From the corner of her eye, Sophia watched Charlie take her cell phone and press the speed dial for Julian.

She had to distract them, so they didn't see! She lifted her head, then stood.

"What do you think you're doing?" Boris growled.

She pointed to the kitchen, then the mess on the floor. She made wiping motions.

"Yes. You clean up this mess." Boris nodded to the man who'd crushed her hand. "Go with her, Chester. Make sure she doesn't try anything funny."

"I will clean up the mess," Alena announced.

"No. You and I are going to have a little talk, Alena," Boris said, sticking the gun in her face. He nodded at Sophia. "Go ahead and clean up your mess."

She made her way into the kitchen where she grabbed the roll of paper towels and a trash bag. If only she could find a weapon. Something. Anything.

"Hurry up. We don't have all day." Chester's voice had already haunted her. Now it would forever terrify her.

She clutched the roll and trash bag to her chest and turned back to the living room.

Sweet Jesus, help us, please.

"Detective Julian Frazier." He held the phone against his ear.

Nothing.

"Hello."

Muffled sounds.

He checked the caller ID. "Charlie?"

In the distance over the connection, he heard a man's voice. "Now, Alena, where is the costume, and don't make me hurt you again."

Ice ran through Julian's veins.

"What is it?" Brody asked.

Julian put the cell on speaker, but pressed the mute button. "It's Boris and Milton. They're at Alena's."

"Let's go." Brody ran toward the parking lot, calling for backup as he did.

Julian kept a tight hold on his cell phone as he followed his partner to the car.

"I do not know." Alena's voice warbled, but was strong.

"You don't want me to hurt you in front of your *vnuchka*. She already saw her mother killed over this costume. Surely you don't want her to have more heartbreak."

Julian's right hand balled into a fist.

"Look how nicely she has healed, Alena. You don't want us to have to break her up again, do you?"

Julian gritted his teeth.

"I did not say you clean up the mess, translator. Sophia can clean up her own mess."

At least Sophia was alive.

"She can't. Not with the injuries you inflicted on her last time." Charlie was defiant, as always. Was she trying to get herself killed? "Let me do it. Then maybe you can tell me exactly what it is you want, and I can help you find it."

"Fine. You clean up, then you help us. Sophia, you sit here, by your *Babushka*."

"Charlie's stalling them to give us time," Brody said.

Julian nodded. "We can't go in hot. If they hear the sirens, they'll kill them all. We've got one shot at this."

Brody grabbed the radio mic and gave the order for silent approach. He also requested emergency medical dispatched as well.

Julian pulled his gun from his holster and held it. The cold metal comforted his throbbing pulse.

"They're going to be okay, Julian. God's got them."

If only he could be so confident . . .

Okay, God. If You're there and listening, please keep them safe. Take care of them right now, until we get there.

"Maybe you are the smarter generation, eh, Alena? You got out of Mother Russia, too."

"I left for my daughter. To give Nina chance to be best ballerina in the world."

"Yes, Nina was beautiful dancer. My brother loved her, you know. He really loved her. When she disgraced herself with . . . the American, he was disgusted with her. Giving her body to an American when she had denied Dimitri."

"My Nina was pure. The American took advantage of her heart."

Julian could only imagine how Sophia felt, sitting there having to listen to such things about her parents. "Can't you drive faster?"

"I'm doing eighty," Brody said as they squealed around another curve. "This road isn't exactly straight and flat you know."

"Nina was a tease. She led Dimitri on, then got pregnant by a dirty American." The man chuckled.

The sound stood the hairs on the back of Julian's neck at attention.

"You don't like to hear the truth about your mother, eh, little Sophia? Maybe I should show you what real Russian man is like."

Julian was going to kill him.

"Okay, it's cleaned up. Now, tell me what you're looking for, and I'll help you find it." Charlie to Sophia's rescue. Again.

Julian owed her big-time.

"The costume. I need the costume. Tell me where it is, and I will not hurt any of you any more."

No, he'd just kill them.

Brody pushed the accelerator to ninety as they hit a straight-away on the road.

"I'm not familiar with ballet, so you'll have to tell me what the costume looks like."

"Don't play me, translator."

"I-I'm not. I don't want you to hurt me or my friends again." Charlie sounded weak.

Julian knew better. "She's doing good at stalling them, but not provoking them."

Brody nodded. "Has she had any training?"

Julian shook his head and concentrated on listening.

"It is pink costume. A fairy."

"I think I saw it once. At Nina's. It was in the attic."

"No! It is not at the house."

"I'm pretty sure it was in the attic with a bunch of other cos-tumes she had. From her dances. There were a couple of trunks in the attic full of costumes."

"There is no trunk in attic. You are lying, translator."

"No, I'm not. Go look for yourself." The pause only lasted a beat. "Oh, wait. You can't because the house burned down. Did you burn down the house with the costume you want so badly in it?"

Now she was provoking them.

"Almost there," Brody said.

Julian tightened his grip on his gun.

"I told you not to play with me, translator."

"No!"

Pow-pow-pow.

Julian nearly dropped his gun onto the floorboard. *God, please! If You're really there, please help.*

Cries rang out over the phone, but Julian couldn't tell whose.

———— ⁂ ————

Sophia sobbed as she reached for Charlie. Boris grabbed her by the hair and pulled her. "No, no, little Sophia. You should not help her. You must help me."

The pain was as horrible as the first attack. They were going to die here. Now. Her. Alena. Charlie.

All because of her and her mother's need to provide her with the gymnastic training she'd selfishly soaked up.

Lord, I'm so sorry. They wouldn't be in danger if it weren't for me. Please, take me but save them. They don't deserve this.

She stood and faced Boris and Chester Milton. She stuck out her chin, just like she'd seen Charlie do.

Boris's eyes narrowed. "You dare to defy me as well?"

He leveled the gun at her.

Sophia closed her eyes. *Take me home, Jesus. I want to see* Mamochka *and my father with You in heaven.*

A gunshot rang out.

Sophia felt nothing. Wow, this wasn't the painful experience she'd imagined.

Thud!

She opened her eyes to find Alena at her feet, eyes open in death.

"Stupid woman jumped in front of the girl," Chester growled.

"Doesn't matter. It ends now anyway. Dimitri was clear. We are to kill them all and burn this place as well, and it will all be over." Boris raised the gun again, leveling it at her head. Then, everything happened at once:

Charlie sprang up off the couch and lunged into Boris.

The gun went off, the bullet driving into the wall.

Boris and Charlie both fell to the floor.

Chester Milton grabbed Boris's gun and pointed it at Sophia.

The front door crashed open. Julian and Brody jumped into the room.

Brody tackled Chester Milton.

And Julian caught Sophia just as the room tilted and spun.

Then darkness enveloped her.

19

Beep. Beep. Beep.

The sound was truly annoying.

And familiar.

Sophia blinked open her eyes to find Charlie standing beside her bed. "Hey, there. Welcome back. I was about to wonder if you just had a thing for hospitals."

"How? I thought you were dead when he shot you," she mouthed.

"Yeah. The bullet barely grazed my shoulder." She pulled down the collar of her shirt to reveal a two by two square of gauze. "Didn't even need stitches. Anyway, when he nicked me, I realized he might think he killed me if I slumped over and played dead."

"You saved my life," Sophia mouthed.

"Yeah. I did. You owe me." Charlie grinned and winked at her.

"Alena?"

Charlie went sober and shook her head. "I'm sorry. She didn't make it."

"She jumped in front of the bullet for me."

"I know." Charlie reached out and squeezed her shoulder. "She made the choice to sacrifice her life for you."

"After wanting me to have been aborted, she gave her life for mine." Sophia didn't miss the irony.

"She did the right thing," Charlie whispered.

But she was just as dead as *Mamochka*. When would the dying ever end?

"Julian?" she mouthed.

"Is a hero, of course." Charlie grinned.

"What's going on?"

"Well, from what Julian and Brody told me, while they arrested Boris Taras and Chester Milton and have plenty of evidence to put them away for a long time, what they said at Alena's—what Brody and Julian heard on the phone—implicates Dimitri Taras's involvement in multiple crimes."

Like her mother's murder.

"While Dimitri lives in New York, records show his plane left there and filed a flight plan to land in Memorial Field Airport in Hot Springs in less than an hour. They're trying to keep everything hush-hush to catch him."

"Like that worked out so well the first time."

Charlie laughed. "I know, right? Anyway, Julian, looking all menacing and bad boy, is cooling his heels at the station where they hope Dimitri will be soon."

Sophia grinned. She could so see Julian looking like that.

But she was just a witness in his case.

"What's wrong?" Charlie asked.

"Nothing."

"Hey, I saved your life, remember? You owe me. Spill it."

Sophia took a deep breath. "I know you tried to warn me not to get attached. I'm just in a case he's working, and it's natural for me to see him as a hero and feel some sort of attraction to him . . . but I can't help it."

Charlie glanced at the floor. "Yeah, about that." She lifted her gaze to meet Sophia's. "I was wrong. Well, no, what I told you is true, it does happen all the time, but not this time. I'm not saying he isn't a hero—" She shook her head and smiled. "Let me try this again. I shouldn't have said anything to you. It's none of my business."

"No, it's okay. You're right. I'm just saying even with your warning, my stupid heart won't listen. Every time I see him, or hear his voice . . . heck, even just hear his name, my heart goes crazy. When he walks into the room, butterflies go spastic in my stomach. I try to tell myself to stop it. That he's just doing his job, but for some reason, my heart isn't listening." Sophia couldn't believe all that had just spilled out.

"Because your heart is smarter than your head, and smarter than me, too."

Now Sophia was confused. "What do you mean?"

Charlie groaned. She lowered the bedrail and sat beside Sophia. "I've made a mess in something, and it was never my business in the first place."

"It's okay."

"No, it's not. I stuck my big nose where it didn't belong, and I think I messed things way out of whack."

Sophia touched Charlie's hand. "It's okay."

"I think Julian is just as attracted to you as you are to him. I basically warned him off of you, too. I told him you were vulnerable and he could hurt you, so to not mess with your emotions. I'm so sorry, Sophia."

"No, it's okay. You were only trying to protect me. I appreciate it." But her mind spun. Could Julian have feelings for her? If he did, what did it mean for them? Could they have a chance?

"I feel awful, and to make up for it, I'm going to tell you a little bit about Julian that I normally wouldn't. I just want you to have a full picture before you decide if you should follow your heart or not, okay?"

Sophia nodded.

"I met Julian through my brother, Scott. He's a mechanic, and a good one. Scott had a friend, Eli, who introduced Scott to his partner who was working on fixing up an old car." Charlie shrugged. "It's a guy thing, I don't know."

Sophia smiled, remembering the affection Julian showed "Maggie."

"Anyway, the friend was Julian. Those three must have worked on the car forever. Seemed like every time I went by the garage to see Scott, Eli and Julian were there. I used to pick on them about they must not be good detectives since they were always working on those old clunkers."

Three years—that's how long Julian said it had taken him to restore his Charger.

"Because Scott's deaf, I learned to read lips when we were kids. Used to drive my parents crazy because we could shut them out of a conversation since they never mastered lip reading. One day, at the shop, he and I started talking, but actually lip reading, back and forth pretty fast. Julian mentioned it might be helpful to learn how to read lips in his line of work. We began discussing how a lip reader could help out the force. Thus, my assignments from them began." Charlie shifted on the bed. "I tell you all this to let you know I love Julian a lot. He's done a lot for me and for Scott, and I would never want to see him hurt. He's like another brother to me."

"I understand," Sophia mouthed.

Charlie let out a heavy breath. "When Eli was killed in the line of duty, something inside Julian snapped. He changed. I could almost see him physically withdrawing from everyone and everything. Except work. He buried himself in the job. I tried to tell him he shouldn't. I begged him to go back to the department's therapist. He wouldn't hear of it." Charlie ran a hand through her tangled hair.

How hard it must have been on Julian. His partner, his best friend, killed. Much like what Sophia felt about losing her mother, having her murdered right there beside her.

"He pushed me away. Scott away. God away. Oh, he'd never been a religious zealot, not by any means, but he believed in God. He'd go to church with Eli almost every Sunday. But after Eli was gone, instead of turning to God for comfort, he turned away in anger."

Sophia knew she'd never get through everything if she didn't have her faith to lean on. If Julian had nothing . . . her heart broke for him.

"He rebelled. I invited him to go to church with us, but he refused. Not politely either. Needless to say, Julian's got some broken parts in him." Charlie gave Sophia's arm a squeeze. "But since you came along, I see those walls he's built up coming down. Not crumbling in one fell swoop, you understand, but bricks slipping out of place. I think you could be the one to reach him, but I don't want you to take him on as a project. Don't think you need to fix him. You can't."

"I can pray for him."

"Yes. I do. Every day."

"I've been mad at God before. I know how it feels. But I also know how it feels to be welcomed back into our Father's arms. To find the love and comfort there. I want the same for Julian, no matter how our relationship shakes out."

Charlie leaned over and hugged her. "You're a special woman, Sophia Montgomery."

"And so are you."

Charlie hugged her again, and Sophia closed her eyes and melted into the embrace. She couldn't remember ever having a friend who was as dear as Charlie. She liked it. A lot.

Almost as much as she liked being around Julian Frazier.

"They got him!" Brody exploded into the room. "They're bringing Dimitri in now."

Julian smiled. Now the fun would begin. So far Boris had remained silent, not giving up his brother. But now with Dimitri on his way . . .

"Come on, let's go let Boris know his brother will be here shortly."

Brody followed him to the interrogation room. Julian took his customary seat opposite Boris while Brody hulked against the wall near the corner.

"Thought you might like to know Dimitri is on his way here, Boris."

For a split-second, Boris's guard came down allowing Julian to see the wariness in his face. A second later, the stony expression was back in place.

Julian would use it. "You know, we have enough forensic evidence to bury you for Nina Montgomery and Alena Borin's murders. Combined with Sophia's testimony of the assault, you'll be lucky not to get the death penalty."

Boris blinked three times in rapid succession.

Yeah, he had his attention now. Julian continued. "Both myself and Detective Alexander heard what you said to Alena, Charlie, and Sophia. We're witnesses to your statement that Dimitri is involved." He turned and nodded at Brody. "Can you remember the exact words?"

Brody stepped out from the darker corner and took a seat beside Julian. "I do, Detective Frazier. I wanted to make sure I had it right in my statement. Boris here said, 'Dimitri was clear. We are to kill them all and burn this place as well and it will all be over.'"

Boris went to blinking again.

Julian pounced. "So with your testimony, Dimitri will be charged. His own brother will be responsible for incriminating Dimitri." Julian propped his elbows up on the table. "Do you think he'll be upset with you? Hmm." He twisted to look at Brody. "Would you be mad at me if I ratted you out and you went to prison for a long, long time?"

"I didn't rat him out. You were eavesdropping." Boris finally broke his silence.

Inside, Julian cheered. Once communication started, the floodgates usually followed. "But Dimitri won't know." He smiled. "And we sure aren't going to tell him any different, are we, Detective Alexander?"

"Nope. Not me."

"You cannot do this. You cannot lie like that."

Julian grinned bigger. "Yes, we can. And we will."

"Unless you give us a statement. Tell us the whole story and we'll tell the judge how you helped us," Brody said.

"I will not go to prison?"

"Oh, you're going to prison," Julian said. He'd like nothing more than to beat him to a bloody pulp, but at least he'd make sure this creep went to prison for the rest of his life.

"But maybe you won't get the death penalty. And we can ask the judge to keep you in a different prison than your brother."

"To keep you safe." Julian leaned back in the chair and crossed his arms over his chest. "The choice is yours, Boris, but only if you talk now. Dimitri will be here in a few minutes, and once he's here, the offer is gone."

It took Boris all of three minutes to decide to sell out his brother. "I will tell you everything."

Julian turned on the recorder, and Brody stepped out to make sure Captain Pittman and another officer were in the observation room.

"Okay, tell me about Nadia Paley's murder."

Boris licked his lips. "Two nights before she came to Arkansas to perform, she met with my brother—"

"Your brother, Dimitri Taras?"

"Yes. Dimitri. She met with Dimitri and told him she was pregnant with his baby. She demanded he marry her. He told her to get rid of the baby and not to throw away her career like Nina Borin had."

Julian struggled to remain expressionless. They hadn't known Nadia was pregnant.

"She told him no and left. He was furious."

"I can imagine. After all, he'd seen Nina's career die as soon as she quit dancing to have Sophia," Brody said, egging Boris on.

"Dimitri flew to Little Rock for her performance—"

"But he wasn't listed as being on the flight on the passenger list," Julian interjected.

"No, of course not. Dimitri was the co-pilot. No one on the plane saw him except for the pilot."

Sneaky. Very clever.

"So he went to see Nadia . . ." Brody prompted.

"Yes. He said her performance was the best ever. After the ballet, he snuck backstage where she had changed. He said her costume was on the back of a chair. They argued. He never meant to kill her, only make her either agree to get rid of the baby or make her lose it. She scratched his face then flung her costume at him. It hit him in the face. He said he remembered wiping the blood on her costume, then slamming it back on the chair."

Which explained how his blood droplets were on the costume.

"He said he pushed her, and she fell backward, hitting her head on the chair and knocking it over as she fell," Boris continued. "He said she died as soon as she hit the floor. He was going to clean it up, but he heard people in the hall, so he grabbed his coat and left."

Wow. Murder and escape. And he'd gotten away with it for sixteen years. Probably never would have gotten caught had it not been for the blackmail.

Julian pushed him. "When did the blackmail start?"

"About a year later. Dimitri received a letter instructing him to wire fifty thousand dollars every year to this same account. The letter told him they knew what he'd done and had proof. Said wouldn't it be hard for him to explain how his blood got on Nadia's costume she wore just before she was murdered. And it included the picture of the costume, with blood clearly on it."

Julian struggled with this one. Nina had obviously broken the law by blackmailing Dimitri, and if she were still alive, he'd be charging her. How would Sophia feel about it?

Then again, if she were still alive, he probably wouldn't know Sophia, so how she felt wouldn't matter.

The realization stung. He couldn't imagine not knowing Sophia.

"He paid the money, every November. He tried to trace the account, but the wire transfers were too complicated. He just resigned himself to pay fifty thousand dollars a year for the person's silence. After more than a decade, he never doubted they would keep their word and not tell anyone."

"But it all changed?" Brody asked.

Boris nodded. "In his mind, she was his true love. He wanted to keep tabs on her so he could swoop in and make her love him if he ever got the chance. One day, he gets the call her name is mentioned in a newspaper article. The investigators send it over. He is shocked and outraged when he sees the picture and recognizes the costume."

That did have to hurt. The woman you believed was your true love having blackmailed you for over seven hundred and fifty thousand dollars.

"He is livid. Furious. Figured out she must have been at the ballet and saw what happened, then stole the costume to blackmail him. He calls me to take care of this for him. Of course, he is my brother, so I agree."

A knock sounded at the door. Julian stood. "You two go ahead. I'll be back." He stepped out of the room.

Captain Pittman met him in the hallway. "Dimitri Taras is here."

20

It'd been a long, long time since he'd been in a church.

Well, Julian considered, it wasn't a church, but a hospital chapel. Still he felt God's presence here with him. Sitting in the front row, staring at the stained glass depiction of Jesus on the cross.

"It's me, God. Julian." He groaned. As if God didn't know who he was.

He shook his head and tried again. "I wanted to thank you for watching over Sophia and Charlie. I was scared for the first time since Eli died." Just saying his name aloud scraped against his heart.

"I'm sorry for being mad at you about Eli, God. I was so hurt he was gone. I lashed out at you because . . . well, because you're God." He smiled. Surely, God had a sense of humor. Seriously, look at porcupines . . . God *had* to have a sense of humor.

"I didn't even realize how much I loved Eli until he was gone. I had to blame somebody, and you were the easiest target. I'm so sorry."

A lump the size of Little Rock lodged in the back of his throat.

"I'm sorry for a lot of things, but mostly . . . well, I'm sorry for trying to pretend You didn't exist. I know denying You is one of the big sins. I'm so sorry, God. Please forgive me."

Tears built in his eyes.

He ducked his head and closed his eyes. "I'm so sorry, God," he whispered.

Almost physically, Julian felt a warm wave shudder through his body. Without reason, he just knew everything was okay. It was okay. He was okay.

"Julian?" the voice was like an angel's.

He stood and slowly turned, finding Sophia standing at the chapel's entrance.

⸱⸱⸱⸱

The way he stood in the light made him appear to glow.

"Sophia?" He closed the distance between them. "What? How?"

She lifted one of her fingers to his lips. "Shh. Brody told me where I might find you." Her breath wouldn't behave.

"Your voice . . ."

"Dr. Rhoads said I need to limit how much I talk for the next few days, but my vocal chords are fine. No permanent damage."

"I have so much I want to tell you . . . so much to share with you." His smile went all the way to his eyes. "But first, I have to tell you, I think you are the most extraordinary woman I've ever met, and I want to take my time getting to know you better, if you'll let me."

She couldn't trust herself to speak, so she nodded.

He wrapped his arms gently around her waist and drew her to him. Slowly, with his eyes never leaving hers, Julian leaned into her. She closed her eyes and felt the soft caress of his lips brushing against hers. Gentle, yet firm. Careful not to hurt her healing cut just above her lip, but thorough enough to spread heat all the way down to her toes.

He pulled back, keeping his arms around her waist, just the space of a breath. His eyes locked onto hers, probing deep into her very soul.

And in that exact moment, her heart danced from her chest to live in Julian Montgomery's capable hands.

Discussion Questions

1. Sophia survived a most violent attack. Have you or someone you know been a victim of violence? Explain how you worked through the myriad emotions afterward.

2. Nina kept Sophia away from Alena. Do you agree with her decision? Why or why not?

3. Julian turned against God after his partner died. Has your faith ever been tested in such a way? Explain how you resolved your spiritual feelings.

4. Losing her voice, Sophia had to rely on someone else to speak for her. Discuss how you would feel if your independence were restricted.

5. Sophia's dream was crushed when she was attacked. Have you ever had a dream taken from you? How did that make you feel? What did you do?

6. Sophia and Nina shared memories over the quilt. Do you have a quilt that has some special significance to you? Please share.

7. Alena and Nina both made sacrifices for their daughters. Discuss the different motivations for each mother's actions. Discuss their similarities.

8. For Alena and Nina, ballet was a vital part of their lives. For Sophia, that vital part was gymnastics. Do you have something

that's very near and dear to your heart? Do you share it with your family? Discuss ways to create something special with your family.

9. Sophia's family could be considered dysfunctional. Discuss how. Now come up with suggestions for how things could have been different. Share different scenarios and outcomes.

10. Nina never reconciled with her mother, never forgave her. What does Scripture tell us about forgiveness? Discuss what particular Scripture on forgiveness speaks most to your heart. Explain why it does.

Want to know more about author Robin Caroll?
Want to know about other great fiction from Abingdon Press?

Please check out our website at
www.abingdonpress.com
to read interviews with your favorite authors,
find tips for starting a reading group, and
stay posted on what
new titles are on the horizon.

Be sure to visit Robin online!
www.robincaroll.com
www.facebook.com/Author.RobinCaroll

We hope you enjoyed Robin Caroll's *Hidden in the Stars*, and that you'll continue to read Abingdon's Quilts of Love series. Here's a sample of the next book in the series, Jodie Bailey's *Quilted by Christmas*.

1

4 . . . 3 . . . 2 . . . 1 . . ." The small crowd's voice rose in pitch and trembled with the chill as the lights flickered into life on the eighteen-foot tree in the small park in Hollings, North Carolina. Along Main Street, lampposts and white lights popped to life and bathed downtown in a warm glow.

Taryn McKenna shoved her hands deeper into the pockets of her coat to keep from blowing on her fingers again. It only made them colder in the end. What global warming? It felt like every year was colder than the one before. The wind coming off the mountain tonight had a particular bite to it, like it had heard the same news as Taryn and wanted to make sure she felt it inside and out.

"Have you seen him yet?" Her younger cousin Rachel leaned close and did her best to whisper, though over the small crowd it seemed more like a shout.

Even Ethan, Rachel's recently adopted thirteen-month-old son thought his mom's voice was too loud. He pressed four chubby fingers against her mouth with a wet, "Shhh . . ."

For a minute, Taryn forgot she was supposed to be vigilant. She arched an eyebrow so high she could almost feel it touch the knit cap she wore over her shoulder-length dark hair. "It's pretty bad when the baby tells you to keep it down."

Rachel flicked honey-blonde hair over her shoulder and planted a smacky kiss on the little boy's cheek, eliciting a high-pitched squeal. "Come on, Mr. Manners. Let's go down to the fire station and see if we can find Daddy." She headed off to walk the three blocks out of downtown. "And we'll get Aunt Taryn out of the crowd before she can have an uncomfortable moment."

Taryn shoved her hands deeper in her pockets and planted her feet. After Rachel's comment, she should stay right here and let Rachel make the trek back to find her EMT fiancé all by herself. She looked over her shoulder toward her own house, two streets over from the park defining the center of Hollings. If she started walking now, she could have hot chocolate in hand and *It's a Wonderful Life* on the TV in under ten minutes.

Not as if she'd be hiding the way Rachel implied. She'd just be warm and comfortable and out of the crowd jostling her as they headed for the community center where the county's Christmas craft festival was cranking up.

The craft festival. She winced. "Rach?"

Several feet ahead of Taryn, her cousin miraculously heard her and turned around. "You coming?"

"I promised Jemma I'd come over and help with her craft booth." *Jemma.* The name was warm on her tongue. Born of the time her tiny toddler mouth couldn't quite get the *grandma* to work like it was supposed to. Her Jemma. The constant love in her life. As much as she wanted to go home and tuck in under a quilt, Taryn had promised and she wouldn't let her grandmother down. "She's got some quilts she's selling in the community center."

Rachel's gaze bounced between the small brick building at the edge of the park and the fire station, invisible down the street and around the corner, where her fiancé probably waited for her to show up with his chicken and pastry dinner from the little church on, yes, Church Street. "I'll come with you and visit your grandmother for a second. I need to thank her for the cute little fireman quilt she made for Ethan's bed. I can't wait until he sees it on Christmas morning." She hefted her son higher on her hip without missing a step. "Mark is hoping the house will be ready by then so we can take Ethan over after he wakes up and have our first Christmas morning as a family in our own house, even if it's empty of everything but a tree."

"That's the single sappiest thing I've ever heard. And maybe the sweetest."

Ethan giggled like he knew exactly what Taryn had said.

Taryn knew better than to offer to take the boy for some snuggles of her own. This was all still new and joyful to Rachel. Give it a month. She'd be begging for a babysitter, and Taryn would be more than willing to oblige. The way her arms ached to snuggle the wiggling, giggling bundle told her so. She shoved the longing aside and slid sideways between two people. "Excuse me."

"Where did all of these people come from, anyway?" Rachel fell a half step behind her as the crowd thickened to funnel through the double doors into the community building.

"It's Christmas in the mountains and it's tree lighting night. Half of them are tourists."

"Sure enough," said an older gentleman with a Boston accent. "Cold down here is a lot better than cold up north."

"Cold is cold." Taryn smiled into his kind face.

"But here, with all the evergreens and the rolling hills . . ." He breathed in deeply. "Feels like you ought to be able to catch Christmas in a bottle up here. Sell it maybe. It's like Christmas magic."

Okay, right. Because there was such a thing as Christmas magic. Where all your dreams came true. Taryn fought the urge to screw up her lips. Never going to happen. She scanned the crowd again, wanting to spot a familiar face and yet dreading it at the same time. It was miserable being torn in two by your own emotions.

"I know what you're thinking." Rachel was right on top of her, one hand holding Ethan's head to her shoulder protectively. "It will happen for you, too. Who knows, maybe with what you heard tonight . . ." She wiggled her eyebrows.

Taryn knew her expression hardened, just from the way her jaw ached. "No. Don't start."

"You can't hide forever. Especially helping Jemma. If he's looking for you, this is the first place he'll go."

"If he was looking for me, he would have found me before tonight. Frankly, I told Jemma I'd help her before I knew he was in town, and had I known, I'd be home right now avoiding a scene." Maybe she should make an appearance, tell her grandmother she wasn't feeling well, and leave fast. It wouldn't be a lie. Her stomach was tying into deeper knots by the second. If she wasn't careful, the country-style steak Jemma had cooked for dinner might just make an encore appearance. "He won't look for me. He's home to see his family. And I'm not his family."

"You could've been, if you hadn't been so stubborn." Rachel may have meant to mumble under her breath, but it came just as a lull in the crowd's conversation dropped, making it a loud and clear indictment.

Taryn stopped right in the flow of traffic just inside the door and turned to look Rachel hard in the eye. It was a mantra she'd stopped telling herself a long time ago, but hearing it now from her cousin, out loud for the first time, the words fired anger and released pent-up emotions Taryn thought she'd tamed long ago. "What did you just say?" The words bit through the air, hanging with icicles.

"Taryn . . ." Rachel's eyes widened like the eyes of a deer Taryn had once hit heading down the mountain into Boone. She looked just as frozen, too. "I never should have spoken out loud."

"So it's okay to think it?" Was it how everyone saw Taryn? As the poor girl who let the love of her life get away? Waving a dismissive hand, Taryn turned and stalked off as best she could, leaving Rachel frozen in the crowd. Good. She deserved it. All those years she'd had Taryn's back, now the truth came out. The whole mess was Taryn's fault, and even her cousin thought so.

By the time Taryn arrived at Jemma's tables, she was angry and over-stimulated. The crowd was too loud, the lights too bright, and the air too stuffy. More than anything, she wanted to pack a bag, hike up to Craven Gap, and pitch a tent for a week. She huffed into a spare metal folding chair and crossed her arms over her chest, garnering a warning glance from her grandmother, who was chatting with their preacher. Taryn sat up straighter and dropped her hands to her lap. She might be thirty, but Jemma still knew how to put her in her place.

Taryn let herself scan the room, filled with familiar townspeople and stranger tourists alike, but no jolt of adrenaline hit her at the sight of any of the faces. It disappointed and relieved her. Over the past dozen years, she'd managed to bury every emotion about the year deep down, so deep she hadn't realized how badly she wanted to see Justin Callahan.

Despite the longing, a conversation with him couldn't end well. Still, her eyes wouldn't stop searching, even though something told her she'd know if Justin walked in, whether she spotted him or not. From the time she was a child, her heart had always known when he was nearby.

Rachel stood on the far side of the room at Marnie Lewis's booth, which overflowed with all manner of jams and jellies. If she could, Taryn would slip over there and lay her head on Marnie's shoulder, unburdening herself of the tense anticipation knotted in her stomach. Where Jemma was all practicality, her best friend Marnie was the soft shoulder for Taryn's many tears. There had only been once when she'd had to refuse Marnie's comfort, because the secret of those tears would have been too much for the older woman to bear.

But there was no time for pouring it all out now. Taryn shoved out of the rusting metal chair and busied herself straightening the quilts hanging from curtain rods hooked to a painted black peg board. Her fingers ran down the stitches of a red and white Celtic Twist, one of Jemma's latest creations. This one was done on the trusty Singer machine in the upstairs sewing room at the white house in the center of the apple orchard. Tourists loved Jemma's work, so she packed up the quilts she stitched by day and brought them to large craft fairs around Asheville and smaller ones in tiny valley towns like their own. The more tiny Hollings made its mark on the map as a North Carolina mountain tourist spot, the more out-of-towners discovered they had to have Jemma's work. Her Celtic designs practically walked out the door right by themselves.

Taryn ran her hands over a complicated Celtic Knot to smooth the wrinkles as a shadow fell over the fabric. "This one's a beauty, isn't it?" She angled her chin up, ready to put on her selling face to the latest tourist.

Instead, she met all too familiar hot chocolate brown eyes. His brown hair was shorter than she'd ever seen it, though the top seemed to be outpacing the sides in growth. His shoulders were broader under a heavy black Carhartt coat, his face more defined. Every muscle in her body froze even as her stomach jumped at the heat of seeing him. She'd known this day would come, knew he was in town now, but still, she wasn't ready.

Clearly, neither was he. He looked at her for a long moment, opened his mouth to speak, then was jostled by a tourist who stopped to peruse the lap quilts on the small plastic table. "This was a bad idea." Justin shook his head and, with a glance of what looked like regret, turned and blended into the crowd, leaving Taryn to watch him walk away. Again.

"What exactly was that all about?"

When Jemma offered Taryn a ride home as the craft show wound down for the evening, Taryn figured she was safe. After all, Jemma hadn't said one word about Justin's awkward appearance and rapid disappearance. Maybe she hadn't even noticed the entire exchange. In the bustle of answering questions and selling quilts, all she'd asked was if Taryn would come over tomorrow and spend part of her Saturday decorating the Christmas tree and working on Rachel's wedding quilt with her.

But now, as she pulled Taryn's kitchen door shut behind her, Jemma revealed just how much patience she had. About three hours' worth.

Taryn pulled two chunky diner-style coffee mugs down from the white wood cabinets and thunked them onto the ancient butcher block countertop. "What's all what about?" It was a long shot, but maybe the question had nothing to do with Justin at all. Maybe this was more about how she'd stalked into the booth and plopped into her chair like a three-year-old in full pout. Taryn rolled her eyes heavenward. *Please, God? I'm not ready to have the Justin conversation yet.*

"The little two-second exchange between you and a man who looked an awful lot like Justin Callahan all grown up."

Nope. It was exactly what Taryn had feared it was about. She yanked open another cabinet and dug out a plastic container of Russian tea. Every year, when the first breath of winter blew along the valley, Taryn mixed instant tea with dried lemonade, orange drink, and spices just like her mother always had. It kept her close, made Taryn feel like she could close her eyes and have her mother reappear whenever she needed her. Boy, did she ever need her tonight. "Want some tea?"

"It was him, wasn't it, Taryn?" The voice wasn't demanding, just gentle, maybe even a little bit concerned.

Demanding would have been better.

Taryn turned and leaned against the counter to find Jemma still by the back door, arms crossed over her red and green turtleneck sweater. "I asked you to come in for something warm to drink, not to answer questions, well, I don't have answers to." She threw her hands out to the sides. "But yes, it was Justin. And why he came over to speak to me, I have no idea."

Jemma nodded, one gray curl falling out of place over her temple. "Looked to me like he wanted to talk to you and thought better of it once he looked you in the eye. Can't say I blame him. You looked scared to death."

Yeah. Because she didn't want him reading her mind and ferreting out all of her secrets. She might have done the right thing for him nearly twelve years ago, but it didn't mean he ever needed to know about it. "I was surprised."

"You always knew he'd come home someday. I'd have never thought it would take him this long. The Army's kept him pretty busy, I'm guessing."

"He's been stationed overseas a lot. Too far to come home often. When he has been home, he's kept to Dalton on his side of the mountain. I'm pretty sure he hasn't been to Hollings since we were in high school." The minute the words left her mouth, Taryn wished she could pull a Superman and make the world spin backwards just long enough to stop herself from saying them in the first place.

Jemma's eyebrow arched so high it was a wonder it didn't pop right off of her forehead. "You kept track?"

"I'd run into his mom occasionally. Rarely. Every once in a while." Awkward encounters for Taryn, because Ellen Callahan was always so friendly, so open, as though Taryn and her son hadn't flamed out in a screaming match in their front yard the night before he left for basic training. While she told Jemma almost everything, she'd kept those brief conversations a secret. The less they talked about Justin, the better, because talking about him kept her from pretending anything ever happened.

"I'll have some Russian tea." Jemma finally answered the long-asked question, then pulled a spoon from the drawer by the sink and passed it to Taryn. "You're going to have to talk to him sooner or later."

Taryn dug the spoon into the fall leaf-colored powder and dumped it into a mug. "I never plan to talk to him. At least not the way you're implying. And aren't you the one who told me for years not talking to him was the better option?"

A car hummed by on the road in front of the house, loud in the sudden silence of the kitchen. Jemma didn't move, then she shook her head. "Opinions change. Maybe . . . Maybe I was wrong."

"No, you were exactly right. Besides, he's home for Christmas this year, and then he'll be back off to parts unknown in the world. If history is any indicator, he won't be back in Hollings for another dozen years, and by then . . ." She shrugged a *no big deal*. By then, she'd probably still be Taryn McKenna, schoolteacher, living in the small green house on School Street, except maybe she'd have half a dozen cats for company. It was what she deserved, and it was likely what she'd get.

With a long-suffering sigh, Jemma pushed herself away from the counter and ran light fingers down the back of Taryn's dark hair. "It's your choice, but I'll be praying."

Something in her tone froze Taryn's fingertip on the button for the microwave. "Why?"

Jemma let her touch drift from the crown of Taryn's head to the tips of her shoulder-length hair, just like she had when Taryn was a child, then planted a kiss on her granddaughter's temple. "Because I had a little chat with Marnie while you were taking down the booth tonight. You know how she knows everything about everybody."

"And you're nothing like her at all, are you Jemma?" Taryn smiled in spite of the dread. If anyone knew the business of everybody on the mountain, it was her grandmother.

"Don't be cheeky, hon. Your mother and I taught you better."

The spoon clinked against the ceramic of the coffee mug as Taryn stirred her grandmother's tea, the spicy orange scent like a much-needed hug from her mother. The restlessness in her stomach settled. In a couple of weeks or so, Justin would be gone again and she wouldn't have to worry about running into him, wouldn't have to worry about the split in half feeling of wanting to see him, yet wanting to hold him at a distance. "What did Marnie say?"

Jemma pulled Taryn close to her side and pressed her forehead to Taryn's temple. "Justin's not home for Christmas. He's out of the Army. He's moved home to Dalton for good."